Before he lost the nerve, he surged forward again.

Slid urgent fingers into her thick black hair.

Bent to her for a too-necessary kiss.

Arden....

With a little sigh she parted her glossy lips to him, warm and receptive and increasingly, gloriously less poised. She was everything female, milk and magnolias and softness and beauty, and she'd once been his. For a long, blissful moment, life felt like it had before. Back when he'd had a prosperous future to offer and a heritage to be proud of, and what he'd foolishly thought was honor....

Dear Reader,

It's great to be back at Silhouette! One of the more intriguing parts of THE GRAIL KEEPERS books I wrote for the Silhouette Bombshell line was the modern secret society of powerful men. Now in THE BLADE KEEPERS, I get to explore a few of those men.

THE BLADE KEEPERS truly would not be possible without the encouragement and support from several important people. First and foremost, I have to thank the ladies of the Texas Read 'Ems group, who strongly encouraged me to pursue the idea of writing about exiled Comitatus members—and who regularly invite me out of my cave and into the world of book lovers and good food. Then there are my faithful critiquers, including Juliet Burns, Kayli and Toni, and my creative writing students at Tarrant County College, who help remind me every day to write for the love of writing. Finally, to my agent, Paige Wheeler of Folio, and my beloved editor Natashya Wilson, as well as Patience Smith and Mary Theresa Hussey, also of Silhouette Books; you have more faith in me than I sometimes do, and I have no words to convey my gratitude. But I'll try "thank you."

Evelyn Vaughn

EVELYN VAUGHN

Knight in Blue Jeans

Silhouette®

Romantic

SUSPENSE

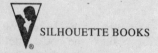 SILHOUETTE BOOKS

Recycling programs for this product may not exist in your area.

ISBN-13: 978-0-373-27635-6

KNIGHT IN BLUE JEANS

Copyright © 2009 by Yvonne Jocks

All rights reserved. Except for use in any review, the reproduction or utilization of this work in whole or in part in any form by any electronic, mechanical or other means, now known or hereafter invented, including xerography, photocopying and recording, or in any information storage or retrieval system, is forbidden without the written permission of the editorial office, Silhouette Books, 233 Broadway, New York, NY 10279 U.S.A.

This is a work of fiction. Names, characters, places and incidents are either the product of the author's imagination or are used fictitiously, and any resemblance to actual persons, living or dead, business establishments, events or locales is entirely coincidental.

This edition published by arrangement with Harlequin Books S.A.

® and TM are trademarks of Harlequin Books S.A., used under license. Trademarks indicated with ® are registered in the United States Patent and Trademark Office, the Canadian Trade Marks Office and in other countries.

Visit Silhouette Books at www.eHarlequin.com

Printed in U.S.A.

EVELYN VAUGHN

believes in many magicks, particularly the magic of storytelling. She has written fiction since she could print words, first publishing a ghost story in a newspaper contest at the age of twelve. Since then, along with her books for Silhouette, she has written four historical romances and a handful of fantasy short stories, some under the name Yvonne Jocks. She loves movies and videos, and is an unapologetic TV addict, still trying to figure out both how to time travel and how to meet up with some of her favorite characters. Even as an English teacher at Tarrant County College SE, in Fort Worth, Texas, Evelyn believes in the magic of stories, movies, books and dreams. Luckily, her imaginary friends and her cats seem to get along.

Evelyn loves to talk about stories and characters, especially her own. Please write her at Yvaughn@aol.com, or at P.O. Box 6, Euless, TX 76039. Or check out her Web site at www.evelynvaughn.homestead.com.

Prologue

One year ago

A voice broke the candlelit hush of the secret society's underground lair. "Nope. I'm sticking with *bite me.*"

The six suits across the ebony table from Smith Donnell tensed with outrage. His three friends, behind him, tensed with more familiar dismay.

"Just speaking for myself," Smith added for their sake.

"And hardly even that," noted his blond buddy, Mitch. "He's kidding— Right, Smith? Ha, ha! Ha. Apologize to the nice society elders and we'll just—"

"But bite me," Smith continued. "This is beneath the Comitatus."

"—commit social and financial suicide," Mitch edited with resignation.

"How dare you?" began Phil Stuart, their overlord. Comitatus leaders were always Stuarts. The Bluetooth headset on one ear made the thirtysomething billionaire look out of place in this stone-lined vault beneath Mount Vernon.

Yeah. *That* Mount Vernon.

"Dare?" Smith challenged now. "We're an *ancient secret society!* We should be as daring as the knights we descended from, not make war on women."

"Not all women," clarified some guy with a French accent. "Only those who prove…problematic."

Smith's friend Trace said, "Oh. That makes it okay, then."

Smith couldn't tell if that was sarcasm or not. Trace was big, not witty.

"Since when do we worry about feminine empowerment?" Smith liked his women saucy—one special woman in particular. But he was understandably biased. "It doesn't hurt us. To start acting like bullies, hiding cowardice behind—"

"Enough!" Stuart slammed his fist on the table, his face flushing to match his red hair. An unnamed society elder behind him—they didn't wear name tags—growled.

"It won't be enough, will it?" whispered Mitch mournfully.

"It never is," Quinn, their fourth, whispered back. The men of Donnell Security had known each other since college. They understood Smith's temper.

Smith folded his arms, scowling. "Didn't the Comitatus once *defend* the weak and the righteous? You act like we're just another old boys' network protecting our exclusivity. Our racial, financial and sexual… I mean…"

He shifted his weight, annoyed. "Our…" Way to ruin a good tirade.

"Chauvinistic?" suggested Quinn quietly, behind him. None of them were stupid—with the possible exception of Trace. But Quinn was the most intelligent.

"Yeah," agreed Smith with a finger jab. "Chauvinistic exclusivity."

"You pledged loyalty to your overlord," warned Stuart. "I, not you, decide the proper course for the Comitatus. Your job is to obey me."

Obey? Smith could hear Mitch whispering, "Let it go, let it go, for the love of all things precious…"

"*My job* is to defend the society that brought honor into my life. I won't watch fearmongers destroy the greatness we once had. *Allegedly* had."

"You pledged your *life* to me," insisted Stuart, leaning across the table into Smith's space. "Your fortune, your sacred honor." Like their fathers before them, and their fathers' fathers, blah blah blah.

"Nope." Smith didn't flinch. "I pledged myself to your uncle. He made a much better leader than you have. You? Kind of suck."

The moment stretched, pregnant with *oh-no-you-didn't.* By challenging the succession, Smith had just finished himself with the society. That imagined rumbling noise was probably his fathers' fathers spinning in their graves.

Was heresy really a killing offense in the Comitatus? Smith tensed, just in case. But he ran a booming business judging threats, and sure enough—

"Get out," commanded Phil Stuart through his teeth.

"Gladly." Smith turned and walked, trusting his friends to watch his back.

"Don't take your knife," warned their overlord as Smith approached the rack where all Comitatus members left their traditional weapons—showy, long-bladed knives—upon entering any ritual meeting place. The two men guarding it squared their shoulders in preparation for a fight. It might be fun, but…

"We used to use swords, you know," Smith called over his shoulder as he passed, just to be contrary. "Back when our honor meant something!"

Assuming it ever really had.

The last thing he heard before the heavy doors shut behind him was a deep growl—and Phil Stuart asking his partners, "And where do *you* stand?"

Hell. No matter what Mitch, Trace and Quinn chose, this had the makings of an awkward ride home. Smith jogged angrily up worn stone steps once trod by George Washington, freemasons and other Comitatus. High-tech security—a system Smith had updated himself—presented a stark contrast to the ancient setting, like the society itself. The modern Comitatus had infiltrated all levels of business and politics. It was a powerful and long-lived organization. Legend held that it had once been great.

Smith had believed in that greatness. But now…

He had barely reached the hidden garden exit behind the ornate tomb before Mitch caught up to him. Trace followed like an oversized shadow. Neither friend carried a ceremonial knife. They'd abdicated their positions, too.

Smith hated like hell to apologize, but… "I'm sorry."

"About our fortunes?" demanded Trace as they walked, putting distance between themselves and any guards. They'd all just made some deadly enemies, after all, which explained Trace's sneer. "Or just our lives and sacred honors?"

Smith looked from one friend to the other—and realized Quinn wouldn't be following them. *Hell.* "Your honor's alive and kicking. You didn't have to fall on your swords to prove it."

"You mean, fall on our knives." Mitch's grin was even brighter than his hair. "Oh, well. Belonging to a secret cabal of ultimate power just isn't what it used to be. I mean, even Trace would have drawn the line at hunting down women."

Trace nodded in big, sullen agreement. Then he frowned. "Hey!"

And there they stood, waiting for Smith, suddenly their leader, to say what happened next. As if he had any idea, beyond…*bad.* Bad, bad things. They'd been born into this society. They'd taken oaths at the age of fifteen. And now…

"What say we get drunk?" he suggested, to their certain approval.

Drunk was the only way he would manage what he had to do next.

It was the only way to say goodbye to Arden Leigh.

Chapter 1

"Beauty is power; a smile is its sword." —John Ray,
English naturalist

Arden was so busy with her hostess duties that she didn't
notice the small exodus until her guest of honor pointed it out.

"I can always tell I'm back in the South," drawled gubernatorial candidate Molly Johannes, "when certain menfolk
head off to talk on their own."

Then Arden saw it and silently cursed herself. True, she'd
had to monitor the needs of her guests, the caterers and the
string quartet. That was why she hadn't bothered with an es-
cort tonight. Her late stepmother had done such an excellent
job with such functions, Arden didn't want to disappoint her
memory. And true, men often drifted away to private conversation in their social circle—a common holdover from the
days of brandy and cigars. But Arden expected better than
"common," especially from her father.

Her first thought was, *Well, sugar. Sugar* meaning something nastier.

But she simply smiled her Miss Dallas smile, complete with dimples, and covered for the men. "As long as they're talking about how to make you governor, Comptroller Johannes, I wouldn't hold their little rituals against them."

"Call me Molly, please! State Comptroller is a mouthful even for the state comptroller." The stocky, middle-aged woman shook her head with amusement. "I'm still not sure why an old boys' club like your daddy's is willing to support me, though I suspect you had something to do with it. But as long as they believe in my message, I'm willing to grant them as much time in their clubhouse as they want."

Arden laughed with her. But as soon as she got Molly talking to another guest, she took a moment to slip out back, into the shadowy August heat of her father's gardens. The clink of wineglasses and murmur of conversation faded like the brightly lit rooms as she let the French door swing shut behind her—and glimpsed, just for a moment, a twinkling of light across the darkness.

She blinked. It had been years since Dallas County had seen many fireflies outside the botanical gardens. Highland Park—a small, exclusive city surrounded by the larger sprawl of Dallas—had plenty of landscaping and parks, and yet…

The air-conditioned chill of indoors faded off her bare arms as Arden scanned the stone paths, the swimming pool, the magnolia and live-oak trees, all the way back to the estate's old well. The light didn't repeat.

She noted the steady glow from what had once been a guesthouse but now was her father's detached study. Shadows moved behind the shades—the usual deserters from her soiree, no doubt. So she headed toward the detached den to sweetly bully her father and his friends back into their public responsibilities.

Which is when a dark-haired, dark-suited young man

emerged from behind the trunk of the nearest oak. That alone startled her, even before she registered the huge hunting knife in his hands.

Really. A hunting knife paired with a Ralph Lauren suit.

Only the unreality of it explained how easily she folded her bare arms, cocked her head and narrowed her eyes. "So much for Daddy's top-notch security," she drawled in accusation. "Whatever do you think you're doing?"

The extra long serrated blade made her stomach go all knotty and sick. But breeding, and her former experience in pageants, gave her skill at hiding her feelings, especially around a man younger than her twenty-five years.

Also? Fear had nothing on her annoyance.

"You need to go back inside the house now," ordered the young man. He wore a small goatee and a had Yankee accent. Massachusetts, she recognized with an even greater flare of surprise. Unless she was mistaken, and roving bands of Bostonians had migrated down to the Lone Star State for a surprisingly well-dressed crime spree, this was one of her *guests!* But how had she not caught his name?

Now she *did* speak her mind. "You come to my party, drink my champagne, eat my hors d'oeuvres and now you *threaten* me? Why, that's just…tacky."

"You think I'm joking?"

"My father and half of Texas society are just a scream away."

Menace twisted his mouth. "Like they'd hear you through closed doors."

"Oh…" Arden smiled, deliberately showing dimples as she bared her perfect teeth at him. "They'll hear me."

He stepped even nearer, so close that she could smell his aftershave—Armani Black—and count the teeth on his knife's serrated blade. Now would be an excellent time to scream, but he said, "Your research and prying have caused enough trouble already."

Which distracted her. Her *research?* That could mean only one thing, and Arden's lips parted in amazement. Suddenly this strange intercession made weird sense. "You mean, it's *true?* There really *is* a secret society of powerful—"

The knife, cold against her throat, confirmed her guess.

Yay?

"If you're smart, you will never refer to such a thing again," Boston warned, making sure Arden could feel the toothy knife above her triple strand of evening diamonds. She tried very hard not to swallow. She could barely breathe. "You will go on behaving yourself, and hosting your little parties, and doing your little charity works. And if you're a good girl, and stay out of matters that don't involve you, *perhaps*—"

Then he dropped.

That would be from the arc of an unexpected tree branch, ending in a sick crack against his head.

The knife landed beside Arden's perfectly pedicured foot. A brown-haired man sank to one knee, strangely like a courtier about to propose, to check Boston's pulse with one hand. Unconscious like that, Arden's attacker looked increasingly young.

Her rescuer kept the tree branch. He looked up, met her gaze—and recognition stabbed through her. Arden knew that angle of brows over mischievous brown eyes, and the sullen-cowboy set to his jaw. She knew the toffee-brown hair by touch, as well as sight. She knew that easy, athletic body, although he'd once dressed far better than his current jeans and dark, long-sleeved tee—a suspicious fashion choice for August in Texas.

But it wasn't just recognition that made her feel even more unsteady than she had with a knife to her throat.

"Smith." The name of the man who'd broken her heart by dumping her without explanation. The man who'd simply vanished from her world.

The man she'd once thought she would marry.

No, what cut the deepest was her recognition, from how her pulse sped up and her breath caught—that she wasn't nearly as over the bastard as she'd hoped.

Oh…*sugar.*

Smith Donnell grinned as he rose to stand taller than her despite her heels, branch in one hand and Boston's knife safe in the other. "Hey, Arden," he greeted cheerfully, as if they'd just run into each other at the club. As if a stranger hadn't just threatened her. *As if he had any right to be cordial!* "How've you been?"

For a minute, Smith feared that Arden might faint. Or maybe she would attack him with balled fists and harder words. She'd always been a lot more of a firecracker than her poised, beauty-queen looks let on—and she was gorgeous, especially in a green gown that matched her wide eyes, with that thick, Irish-black hair drawn off her slender neck, showing all that peaches-and-cream skin….

Smith forced himself to keep breathing. If he were a lesser man, he might have gone a little wobbly himself. And he'd known there was a possibility of seeing her tonight, although he hadn't intended to be seen.

She'd had no idea.

Instead of fainting or fists, Arden smiled that adorable, dimpled smile that had always put him on guard. She extended both hands, saw that his hands were busy with weaponry, and made do with an air kiss. "Smith Donnell, as I live and breathe! How long has it been, three years?"

Smith felt his own grin waver at her overestimation, as well as the hauntingly familiar magnolia scent of her. "Barely a year, to tell the truth."

She waved the idea away. "Time flies, doesn't it? I've been right as rain, thank you for asking. Likely you heard that my stepmother passed. That's been even harder on Daddy and

Jeff—you remember my little brother?—than on me. But what about *you?* You're looking…"

Smith waited for her to put a polite-yet-pointed spin on that one. His life since the big defection at Mount Vernon had been embarrassingly hand-to-mouth. Not every powerful businessman in the world belonged to the Comitatus, of course. Just enough of them to keep the occasional "traitors" from getting references, credit or clean background checks.

Go figure. Secret societies sucked when it came to severance packages.

"Fit," she decided brightly, a euphemism if ever he'd heard one. "So whatever brought you into my daddy's backyard, where you ought not to be, just in time to play knight in shining armor against…?"

As if in an afterthought, she nudged the suited shoulder of her attacker with her strappy dress shoe. Her full lips pulled into an adorable pout of annoyance. He could spend all night just watching her pout. He used to deliberately provoke it.

"I believe his name's Lowell," Smith admitted. No wonder the Comitatus had wanted Donnell Security for their special crusade a year ago, with incompetents like this running around. Lowell had been just plain stupid, going straight for the threats…but then again, the threatening and the posturing illustrated Smith's problem with the whole organization. "Though we haven't been formally introduced."

"And yet here you are. Maybe chivalry isn't dead." Her eyes danced at him. "Other than the you-hitting-him-from-behind part."

He shouldn't feel deflated at that. Their split should've cleared up any delusions she had about his never-steadfast honor. But Arden's easy poise still brought out his contrary side. "I would've challenged him to a duel, but I left my fencing foil with my tuxedo."

"Ah, but you still have that sharp wit of yours, don't you?"

Her composure was starting to worry him, and he'd already been worried. Worried enough to come out of hiding when he saw her threatened. Worried enough to risk his entire erased existence and everything he was accomplishing with that invisibility.

"So, uh…what did Lowell here mean about you doing research into secret societies?" He prayed his betrayal hadn't somehow involved her in this.

Rather than reassure him, she wrinkled her pixie nose in that teasing way that used to make his stomach flip. Still did. "Now if I told, it wouldn't be secret, would it? But look at me, chatting away. I really should call security and get back to my *invited* guests." Still, she couldn't be quite that rude; it all but went against her religion. "Why don't you come inside and have something to eat? Jeff's away at camp, but Daddy will be just *thrilled* to see you again."

Her ability to spout social lies the size of the Watergate cover-up still amazed him. "Haven't you got a hot date to get back to?"

"Three," she assured him, not missing a beat. He half believed her. "But you won't be in our way."

"Actually, sweetness," he said, satisfied at her almost-wince over the endearment, "you'd be doing me a favor if you didn't mention me being here at all." He pressed the branch into her hands. "Or, at least, don't tell anyone my name. I can't say why, just now, but…"

She arched a perfect brow. "But I owe you?" They both knew that, with the way he'd dumped her, he would have to save her life several times before they were even. Still, she had the grace to pretend. "I never could say no to you, could I?"

"Actually, you could." He'd never worked so hard to catch a woman in his life—and then he'd had to go and throw her back, right before he'd meant to seal the deal. Her perfection had been her only flaw. Of all the things he'd lost that night at Mount Vernon… "You really do look fine, Arden Leigh. Always did."

For a moment, her facade faltered. Could that be lingering pain in her big, lash-shadowed eyes? Did she want to kiss him as badly as he did her? Could she be *human* for him, just once more? But the moment passed, and he suspected it was mere wishful thinking on his part.

Not to mention…secrecy and all. Big society plans. Vengeance to be wrought and inner-circle VIPs to betray.

"Give me a count of twenty-five?" he asked, backing away a step. On what should not have been an afterthought, he wiped his prints off the ceremonial knife and flipped it sharply into the manicured lawn, well away from Lowell. When Arden hesitated, eyebrows lifted in challenge, he added, "Please?"

"One," Arden drawled obligingly. "Two…"

Hell. Before he lost his nerve, he surged forward again.

Slid urgent fingers into her thick black hair.

Bent to her for a too-necessary kiss.

Arden…

With a little sigh, she parted her glossy lips to him, warm and receptive and increasingly, gloriously, less poised. She was everything female, milk and magnolias and softness and beauty, and she'd once been his. For a long, blissful moment, life felt like it had before. Back when he'd had a prosperous future to offer, and a heritage to be proud of, and what he'd foolishly thought was honor.

Back when, amazingly enough, he'd had her. After a year without her, to have her so close, so *his,* felt—

Oof! With a sharp jab of the branch into his ribs, Arden put an end to the kiss. Smith felt both relieved and shattered. She stared dazedly up at him, her gaze as raw and resentful as his felt, and he feared the coming accusations, didn't know how he could ever explain himself.

Instead, after regaining her composure with a single, shaky breath despite her hair now falling in messy loops to her bare shoulders, Arden said, "Eleven. Twelve."

Smith ran. It was a big yard. He'd barely vaulted the stone wall before he heard Arden's voice split the night. *"Daddy!"*

In the excitement that followed, Smith had no trouble meeting with Mitch and Trace, whom he'd been signaling with his penlight before Arden's attacker distracted him. As the local Comitatus leadership poured into the garden to Arden's cries, Smith and Mitch stole into the office they'd vacated.

"Niiice." Trace grinned from his position as guard outside. "She's still hot."

"Shut up." Smith punched a code into the security pad with the end of his penlight. The society's new security was top notch, but Smith was better. Mitch was already moving around Donaldson Leigh's dark, heavily furnished den, collecting the surveillance equipment that they'd hidden that afternoon under the cover of all the florists and caterers who'd swarmed the property in preparation for Arden's big night.

"Weird though these words feel leaving my mouth, Trace is right," Mitch admitted, even as he unscrewed a nearly invisible, key logger from Leigh's keyboard cable. "The whole thing had a kind of old-romance, Robin-Hood-and-Maid-Marian look to it."

"Except that this isn't a movie," Smith reminded him, still mulling over the guard's accusation. *Your research and prying have caused enough trouble already.* Arden should have been safe. What had he gotten her into? "Are you done?"

"Almost." Humming a happy little ditty, Mitch stretched to retrieve another tiny, voice-activated microrecorder from a hanging planter. "We're in luck! Nobody watered."

"They won't leave this place empty for—"

"Got it!" Mitch pocketed the recorder and made for the door. "Here's hoping they got to the best plotting and self-implication before Arden interrupted things. Good job stalling her, by the way."

Yeah. That's what Smith had been doing. *Stalling her.*

"Shut up." But instead of running, Smith paused beside what looked like an antique gun safe just inside the door. It wouldn't hold guns. Inside would be at least five long, toothy, ceremonial knives—and suddenly he wanted them.

Rather, he didn't want Donaldson Leigh and the others to have them. The knives represented the society. He itched to challenge that.

Especially when his own father stood with them.

"What happened to low profile?" demanded Mitch, hovering at the closed door. "What happened to nobody knowing we were ever here? Or is Arden going to talk anyway?"

If Arden talked, they might as well add insult to injury and take the knives. It's not like she owed Smith that kind of trust. And yet…

Trace drummed his fingers on the doorjamb. "Guys! Some suits are headed back this way. As long as we're hitting people with sticks tonight…?"

"She won't talk," Smith decided. Hoped. "Not right off, anyway. Let's go before Trace starts a brawl."

Mitch opened the door and Smith tapped in the code to again disable the alarm, careful to leave no fingerprints. The knives, though… Those, he left.

It wasn't like they were swords. It wasn't like they held real value.

Then the three exiles from the most powerful secret society in the world escaped from Donaldson Leigh's property—with what might be the Comitatus's plans to secretly destroy the female gubernatorial candidate inside.

Donaldson Leigh hungered to crack his fist across young Prescott Lowell's jaw. But, no. The Comitatus could not claim to be the apex of civilization while behaving like the un-washed masses.

Instead, he pointed at the boy with his ceremonial knife. "Down."

"But I *had* to threaten her. I was *guarding*—"

"DOWN!" Civilization also depended on *knowing one's place.*

The boy—he couldn't be more than twenty-three—dropped to his knees, defeated. At Leigh's glare, he laid his ceremonial knife on the marble floor in front of him. Whether or not he got it back…

"You were to guard us against our *enemies,* you fool. Not against wandering family members!"

"But…she *knows* about us!" Apparently not content to spout these lies, Lowell actually dared to glare up at his elder.

Leigh used a knee to push the youth onto all fours, then facedown onto the floor. At least the boy knew better than to protest *that!*

"Leigh." Will Donnell drew his friend back with a restraining hand on his shoulder. "I think he understands that he made a mistake."

"But I didn't blow it!" protested Lowell. "I intercepted her—"

"With a *knife!*" At least some of the other elders, behind Leigh, were murmuring agreement at Leigh's complaint.

"She's of the blood. Should I have used a gun?"

Only Donnell's hand on Leigh's shoulder kept him from reacting to such blasphemy as the boy babbled on: "I had to stop her, didn't I? So I *did.* I told her to go back to her party, mind her own business, and she said that there really *was* a secret society!"

Leigh's restraint on his Irish temper cracked. The *hell* with civilization!

Donnell held him back from kicking the boy's teeth in. "Do

you think our families have never had suspicions?" Leigh's friend asked, more calmly. "We have ways to divert them. By confirming them for her, you've caused far more trouble than you prevented."

That, brooded Donaldson Leigh, was an understatement. Certainly more trouble for young Lowell.

And, worse—more undeserved trouble for his beloved daughter, Arden.

Chapter 2

"So he kissed me, and then he just…left."

"And you didn't call the police," noted Arden's friend Valeria Diaz as the women walked through midday heat from a sleekly modern light-rail station into a questionable, once-glamorous Victorian neighborhood. Tall and dusky skinned, her coils of brown hair drawn into a practical ponytail, Val didn't stand out in South Dallas's run-down Oak Cliff neighborhood nearly as much as Arden did.

"The kiss wasn't that bad," joked Arden, before giving in and answering what her friend really meant. "There was no need for the authorities. Daddy said—" She deliberately ignored her friend's roll of the eyes. Especially here in the South, "Daddy" was a perfectly respectable title for one's father…just like it was acceptable to give a boy his mother's maiden name for his first name, as with Smith. "Apparently, Lowell is an intern of my father's. I assumed they would handle the incident internally."

Val's dusky face had all the expression of a stone idol—an idol with intense, topaz eyes. "Someone puts a knife to your throat, he deserves jail time, not a demotion."

Arden's friend and partner never had excelled at girl talk. Val had once, briefly, been a cop. She'd surely been a tomboy. "Daddy has it under control. He's a good man."

"Unlike his daughter, the slut." Val's eyes sparkled with sudden teasing, despite her mask of solemnity. "So you *kissed* this knight in shining timeliness?"

"*Smith* kissed *me,*" Arden clarified with assumed dignity. Then she admitted, "But I didn't exactly bite his tongue." No, instead she'd opened herself to him. His warm touch. His scent of heat and earth. When she should have been skewering his foot with one of her dress heels, she'd instead closed her eyes and pretended—just for a minute—that they'd never broken up. All her foolish, inappropriate longing had gone into that one stolen kiss.

Smith...

Like some desperate fool, she'd started to lift her arms around him, to draw him to her for the first time in too long....

Just as well she'd forgotten the big stick in her hand.

"There was *tongue?*" Val glanced over her shoulder as they walked.

"Smith always did have a peculiar kind of charm." That roguish grin. That cocky indifference. Even during those years when they'd known and disliked each other—or thought they had—she'd sometimes wanted to kiss him just to shut him up.

"Charming as pie, 'til he dumped you."

"Exactly." They turned down a cracked, uneven sidewalk onto a street boasting large trees and more Victorian homes. Several had been renovated to their original elegance, but most sat in graffitied disrepair, with abandoned cars in the front yards and rusting burglar bars on the windows. Historic

Oak Cliff, once a jewel among Dallas society neighborhoods, had fallen victim to postwar white flight and urban decay generations before.

Arden liked to think the recreation center for girls she and Val had started nearby could reverse some of that.

"Dumped you *over the phone*." Again, Val glanced behind them. Satisfied, she turned her stern stare back to Arden. "With no warning."

"Yes, he did."

"Drunk off his butt."

"I was there, Val. *I'm* the one who told *you*."

"Boy deserved biting." Val slid her topaz gaze disapprovingly toward Arden. "And not in any good way."

"Well…I did hit him with a branch."

"Good." But Val knew her too well. "Accident, was it?"

"And I doubt I'll see him again." Which was a good thing, of course.

"Make sure of it, girlfriend."

"Why, look," said Arden brightly, to change the subject. "We're at Miz Greta's."

Miss Greta Kaiser taught piano at the rec center. Her tall stone home, like the neighborhood, had forgotten its elegance beneath decades of neglect. It boasted a mansard roof with uneven iron cresting, dormer windows along the top story, and a high bay window of Second Empire style. Roman arches over its windows and doorway added an Italianate touch. But several of the cracked panes in its higher windows had been patched with cardboard or taped plastic, despite Arden's repeated offers to help with repairs. Lost roof tiles gave the appearance of missing teeth. What must once have been a glorious garden had withered to a brown, dirt-spotted lawn, deprived of sunlight by a single, glorious oak tree and of water by the Texas heat.

It broke Arden's heart to see it. And yet, had the home

joined the ranks of the restored historic houses brightening the area here and there, Miz Greta couldn't possibly have managed its upkeep. The divorcee had macular degeneration, a central blindness that limited her ability to manage certain tasks…which was why she'd asked for Arden's help looking into a suspected secret society. Greta could play piano with her eyes closed. But she could no longer read without a huge magnifying glass.

Today, Arden had brought a new audio book, wrapped in crinkly tissue, for their visit. "It's a hostess gift," she explained to a curious Val after knocking on Miz Greta's recessed door. The expected barking erupted from the other side. Both women took off their sunglasses, and Arden her wide sun hat.

"And I don't get a bodyguard gift because…?"

"Sweetie, you're not my—" But the opening door cut off the rest of her answer. Both women stood a little straighter for their elder. Despite their significantly different backgrounds, both Arden and Val had been raised with Southern manners.

"Please do come in," insisted the small, white-haired woman, braids wrapped around the crown of her head, giving her barely enough height to reach five feet. She peered down at the barking dog through Coke-bottle lenses. "Hush, Dido!" Then— presumably to the women and not Dido—"I've made strudel."

On mere hours' notice? The delicious smell filled the warm house, a testament to Greta's cooking abilities despite her failing eyesight.

"You shouldn't have," demurred Arden as they made their way through the crowded vestibule and into the parlor, because that's what one said. Once she'd presented the gift, she crouched to let the cocker spaniel lick her hand and remember her. Dido wiggled harder at the sheer joy of having company.

"Sure she should," insisted Val, of the strudel.

"I love cooking for guests," agreed the older woman.

In minutes, her visitors had china plates of strudel and tall glasses of sweetened iced tea. Because Greta's old house had no central air—only cheap window units and an assortment of fans that had been running since June—the iced tea was especially welcome, despite Arden's awkwardness at being waited on by someone she'd rather be serving.

Arden felt even worse recounting her adventure of the previous night—but it had to be said, no matter how much it troubled her old friend.

"My God." Miz Greta shook her head, paling at even Arden's most gentle version. "I never dreamed that *you*... You could have been killed!"

"I'm sure I was in no danger." Arden gently squeezed Greta's thin hand. "The Lowell boy was just posturing."

"And apparently Arden's loser ex-boyfriend has miraculous timing," added Val darkly. When the dog barked in the kitchen, she stood.

"Heavens, child! You'll have me jumping at shadows. Dido?" The dog trotted back in and sat, nose pointed at the strudel. "She barks at squirrels."

Val sank back into her chair, but now Arden felt alert, as well. Being recently held at knifepoint had that effect, but it was no excuse for frightening old ladies.

"Dido certainly enjoys company," she noted, a deliberate feint.

"She's very affectionate." The older woman relaxed as she petted her dog. "Hence the name. I've always been partial to Virgil's *Aeneid*. In Roman literature, Dido is the heroine who falls completely in love, then kills herself after her lover deserts her to pursue his destiny."

"Imagine that," murmured Val, no big fan of classic literature—but in the meantime, Miz Greta's cheeks had regained some color from the distraction.

"I wouldn't have mentioned last night," noted Arden carefully, "except that Lowell validated your suspicions. Why would anybody care about our research otherwise? I believe there really may be some kind of secret society out there!"

"A *dangerous* society." Greta shook her head. "Of course you must do as he said and leave the matter be—no need to pursue this further."

"And let them think they've frightened me away?"

"Wait a minute," protested Val. "I came into this late. What kind of secret society are we talking about, and just what kind of research did you do?"

"Not very much," Arden said. "Miz Greta had a…a personal curiosity and asked for my help with some reading. I found a few books about secret societies in general, but this one—they're called the Comi…?"

"Comitatus," provided Greta softly.

"The Comitatus were hardly ever mentioned. I went online to some conspiracy Web sites and posted questions, but almost everyone denied ever hearing of them. Except of course for the teenagers who pretend to know everything but can't tell you anything. Then I found a conspiracy buff who seems to be local—he calls himself Vox07. He offered to meet me with the names of some area members of the society if I would trade information, who knows what kind… That's as far as I got before last night. Why do you keep looking out the window?"

"Never hurts to be careful," said Val. "Especially when— assuming there really is a Comitatus—anyone from a bookstore clerk to this Vox person could have let on that you were asking questions. Way to be stealthy there, Leigh."

Arden resisted the urge to make a face. Val wasn't usually paranoid. She was just…careful.

Arden hated thinking she might have cause.

And why was the dog spending so much time in the kitchen, with company here? Smith had once told her something about dogs and security…. "Where's Dido?"

Neither Greta nor Val understood her non sequitur at first, but Miz Greta called, "Dido! Come!"

The cocker spaniel scrambled happily into the parlor, wiggling her pleasure at being called… But she also cocked her head back toward the kitchen, as if torn. Why?

Dido *loved* company!

"Check her breath," suggested Arden, standing suddenly.

Val was on her feet even before Greta—barely able to hold her exited dog still long enough to open her mouth—exclaimed, "Strudel? Bad dog! How did you get into the—?"

By then, Arden and Val were heading down the narrow, wood-floored hallway past the staircase and library, toward the kitchen—aiming for stealth, which is why Arden had left her pumps back in the parlor. She dropped back a pace only when she saw Val draw a gun from a small-of-the-back holster. Texas had a carry law—and Southern girls were well versed in gun safety, too.

Val practically rolled around the kitchen doorway, weapon first, like the cop she'd once been. She scanned, then crossed the large room with Arden following, past its yawning fireplace and shelves, toward one of three doors. She pushed open one, revealing a second set of stairs blocked with boxes and storage, and shook her head before closing the door to glance back at Arden. "Stairs?" she mouthed in surprise.

"Servants' stairway," Arden whispered back, moving to the 1950s stove to check the pan of strudel. Too much pastry was gone, and it looked like someone had been serving with their fingers.

Dogs make the best security systems. That's what Smith had once told her. *Except for the bribing-with-food part.* He might have driven her crazy sometimes—more often than not, truth be told—but he'd always made her feel safe.

"Someone was here," she said softly.

"What's wrong?" called Miz Greta from the hallway, her

voice quavering in a way that hurt Arden's heart. "Did you find someone?"

"Not that we can see," Arden reassured her brightly. "You just keep hold of Dido and let us make sure, all right?" Careful not to cross Val's line of fire, she stepped to the middle door, this one obviously leading onto the covered porch. Its hook-and-eye latch hung open... Was Greta that lax about security? Around *here?*

Crouching, Arden pushed the door open. Gun first, Val swept the porch.

Again—nobody.

The friends exchanged pregnant glances, torn between amusement at their *Charlie's Angels* routine and the fact that there was one...last...hiding place.

In her stockinged feet, breath shallow from the risk, Arden crossed to the third doorway. Probably the pantry or the larder.

Val held up one finger, to create a count. Then two.

At three, Arden pulled the door open. From behind the shelter it made, she saw Val feint back and shout, "Freeze!"

Dido began to bark wildly—

And a second gun poked past the door as a too-familiar voice, both pleasant and deadly, said, "It's August. This place isn't air-conditioned. I couldn't freeze if I wanted to."

Smith? Arden leaned past the door to peek at the man she'd immediately recognized, both from his voice and from his truly inappropriate sense of humor. His eyes didn't look that mischievous just now, but his jaw was set even more stubbornly than usual—and his aim on her best friend didn't waver.

Val aimed right back.

Over a year with no word, and now Smith had shown up twice in less than twenty-four hours? As ever, Arden took refuge in hard-won composure.

"Hey, Smith," she drawled coolly at the gunman, deliberately imitating his cocky greeting of the night before. "How've you been?"

Chapter 3

W ell.

This wasn't how Smith would've preferred to kick off his next meeting with Arden. Not that he'd actually meant her to see him again. Despite following her here. But…still.

He kept her Latina friend in his sights—mainly because she still had him in hers—but said, "Arden Leigh, as I live and breathe. Seems like forever, huh?" What with them replaying last night and all. Since he didn't want to take his gaze off the lady looking to shoot him, he didn't put a hand to Arden's pretty cheek. Instead, he made do with an air smooch. "Kiss, kiss."

"And here I thought you didn't like guns." How could she put such thick disapproval into such a sweetly phrased statement? She was right, of course. He didn't. But that didn't mean he couldn't hit what he aimed at, or that—after seeing a Comitatus flunky holding her at knifepoint the previous night, and after listening to Mitch's partial recording of the Comitatus agenda—he wouldn't carry one until he knew she was safe.

Which she wasn't, here.

The old lady in the hallway said, "Blades are more honorable than guns, don't you think?"

That surprised the hell out of him, so much that he glanced away from the muzzle of the Latina's Saturday Night Special to the older woman's pale gaze, which seemed to look not just at him but through him. *More honorable.* Those were almost the exact words the Comitatus leaders used when giving a teenaged boy his ceremonial knife upon entry into the society. Blades were personal. Blades were honorable. Guns might be more practical, but if ever someone of Comitatus blood outright betrayed his brethren, he would be shown the honor of dying by blade.

How could she know?

Only when she smiled down at the dog, wizened and wise, did Smith grasp his rookie mistake. The old woman *hadn't* known—not about his own involvement with the Comitatus, anyway—until he'd reacted.

Blades. "Honor's a luxury some of us can't afford," he said carefully.

"Obviously." Arden glanced pointedly between the two guns. "Will you two please put those nasty things away?"

"Her first," said Smith at the same time Arden's friend said, "Him first."

"At the count of three." Arden made it a velvet-gloved order. "One."

The tall, dark woman narrowed her eyes in challenge. "Two."

Smith wished he was staring at Arden instead of a gunwoman. The blue-jeaned Amazon was handsome, in her way. But Arden was pure beauty, and not just because she wore such a pretty sundress, her black hair in a curly ponytail.

Or because her toenails were painted the exact same color as her fingernails and her lips.

Or…

"Three," finished Arden—but the weapons didn't move. She put her hands on her hips, as if she meant business. "Oh, for mercy's sake!"

Smith almost hoped to see her lose her temper—he'd loved catching sight of the real Arden behind the composure since long before they'd started dating.

He *wasn't* ready for her to step right into the line of fire.

Where the slip of a finger could kill her!

"Hey!" Immediately he turned his weapon to the ceiling and thumbed on the safety. His voice cracked. *"Arden!"*

"Are you *insane?*" demanded the other woman, doing the same thing.

"Did I teach you nothing about personal safety?" demanded Smith, struggling to catch his breath. "Never, *never*—"

"NEVER!" insisted her friend.

"I," noted Arden icily to Smith, dismissing the deadly weapons with a roll of her eyes, "am not the one breaking into houses—"

"The door was unlocked, no breaking required."

"—and pointing guns at people. Shame on you!"

The strange thing was, instead of laughing at her, he did feel a touch shamed…which made him petulant. "I was just making sure you weren't into something over your head." Justified, he jabbed a finger in her direction. "Which apparently you *are*. Secret societies and all that…that crazy talk…."

The old lady was staring through him again and smirking. Somehow she *knew* he knew better. He didn't like her seeming omniscience one bit.

Rejecting Comitatus leadership, as he and his friends had done, meant exile. Breaking one's vow of secrecy, on top of the whole dishonor thing, could be one of those nasty, dying-by-blade offenses, depending on the circumstances.

Yet another reason Smith carried a gun today.

All the old lady said was, "Is nobody going to introduce us?"

"How ill-mannered of me." Only Arden could fit so much sarcasm into such proper words or so bright a smile. "Miz Greta, Val, please let me introduce the wholly untrustworthy Smith Donnell. Smith and I have known each other's families since childhood. Once, during a period of temporary insanity on my part, we dated. Smith, these are Miss Greta Kaiser and Ms. Valeria Diaz. Greta teaches piano at my teen recreation center, and Valeria could kill you for fun where you stand."

"Gladly," clarified Val.

"How do you do?" Smith tried his most charming smile. He even bowed a little before seating his revolver back into its SOB holster.

Generally, that was meant as a rhetorical question, but Valeria Diaz said, "Personally, I'm pissed that nobody's dialing nine-one-one yet. And you?"

Torn about what I heard from that Comitatus meeting. Too happy to be in Arden's presence again. Worried about the dark sedan that followed you here from the rail station. "I'm feeling more than a little silly that I chose to hide in a pantry instead of taking a stairway to the whole of upstairs," he admitted, and offered his hand in truce.

Val deliberately ignored it.

"Much as I'm sure you would have enjoyed rifling through Miz Greta's private things." Arden pushed his hand back down to his side, her own hands soft, her scent sweetly familiar. *Thanks for the brush-off, Val.* "I'd rather know why it's your business whether I'm over my head, off my game or out of my mind. There's a great deal I wouldn't put past you, Smith. A *great* deal…" She widened her eyes to think of the enormity of things that included.

"Nice vote of confidence," Smith muttered, to drag her back on track.

It worked. "But *stalking?* Why *shouldn't* we call the authorities?"

None of them expected Greta to step in. "Because if we call the police, Mr. Donnell will miss the story he risked so much to hear. Let's all return to the parlor to deal with the larger issue at hand. Mr. Donnell, would you like some iced tea?"

Val's mouth dropped open in blatant amazement. Arden, being Arden, revealed her surprise with the barest of blinks—but Smith was pretty adept at reading the annoyance of those blinks, and he grinned in pure triumph. Maybe the old lady was crazy, maybe not. But he wasn't one to look a gift horse in the mouth...especially when he'd seen so few gift horses lately.

"Why, *thank you,* Miz Greta. I would love some tea...and maybe a slice of that delicious strudel?" As he accompanied his new favorite person and her gamboling, happy dog toward the front of the house, making the most of his status as a welcome guest, Smith caught Arden's soothing murmur to Val.

"Just take deep breaths, and it will pass. He inspires almost everyone to kill him, sooner or later."

She had no idea how right she was.

The question was, how could someone as perfect as Arden have inspired similar—and all-too-real—threats?

And why was someone with tinted windows parked just down the street, keeping watch on her?

Greta Kaiser was not crazy. Nor was she completely blind, physically *or* emotionally. The macular degeneration gave her *central* blindness. That meant if she looked directly at Smith Donnell, she saw no face at all, barely a head. But she could glimpse, with her remaining peripheral vision, how Arden Leigh snuck peeks at him when she thought nobody was looking. When Greta turned her old eyes on Arden, the beautiful socialite all but vanished—but Greta got a clearer impression of Smith Donnell beside her, a hint of strong profile and brown hair and blatant interest in— almost longing for—someone he had supposedly dumped. He'd managed to sink onto the love seat next to Arden before Val could.

Arden made an amusing show of ignoring his nearness completely.

Greta also noted Smith's worn jeans and T-shirt, his cheap shoes. Put that together with the unlikelihood of Arden having dated someone from a significantly lower social caste— *have known each other's families since childhood*—and Greta found far more truth on the couple's periphery than anyone might by looking at their relationship straight on.

This man may have lost his chance to be Arden Leigh's hero…but he might yet prove to be Greta's.

"My family name," she said, when everyone had finished their bickering and settled back in the parlor, Dido flopped happily between them, "is Kaiser. Does anyone know what that name implies?"

"It's German," offered Arden.

Greta turned expectantly to Smith, even if that meant losing sight of his expression.

"It means 'emperor,' right?" he asked. When Arden and Val stared at him, he seemed to square his shoulders. "What, you think I *bought* my way through college?"

"Yes, 'emperor'." Greta settled back in her favorite chair, comforted by Dido's chin on her foot. "The name derives from the word *'Caesar,'* because the Hapsburg dynasty professed direct lineage to the Roman emperors, themselves descendents of the epic hero Aeneas. Hence our claim to the Holy Roman Empire."

"And you're a Hapsburg?" Arden sat up. "Of the *Austrian* Hapsburgs?"

In periphery, Greta caught the suspicion that began to

darken Smith Donnell's strong profile. He was starting to figure this out already.

Clever. Arden had exceptionally good taste.

"Let us say we are a significant branch off that family tree. As you might guess, my father was a powerful man, descended from a seemingly unending line of powerful men. I was born in this house, back when Oak Cliff was the garden spot of Dallas society. I fully expected a life of private schools, debutante balls and eventual marriage into wealth. But instead…" She took a deep breath, bracing herself against the memories. "Even before my coming out, shortly after World War II, my father lost everything. Our fortune. Our standing. The house—I did not inherit it, only bought it back decades later, after the falling property values made it available for a fraction of its original cost.

"We were wholly ruined, and I never knew why."

Arden leaned forward to take Greta's hand, offering sweet comfort. Greta smiled directly at the black-haired beauty, effectively erasing Arden from her vision but allowing her to glimpse Smith's sudden, wary stillness.

"Well…" He paused, then continued, not quite hiding the sympathy in his tone. "That *would* be terrible."

He, she felt increasingly convinced, should know. If he didn't, she was endangering herself and perhaps Arden and Val—even Dido—by continuing. But life was risk.

"Astute as ever." Arden's poise had degenerated into dry sarcasm. Interesting.

"College," Smith reminded her amiably. But, observing the contrast between his current apparel and the upper-class confidence of his posture, Greta felt sure he'd spoken from firsthand experience.

"Our family never wholly recovered." She could not admit her childish resentment, nor how long into adulthood it had followed her. A foolish marriage, for all the wrong reasons.

A bitter divorce, for the right ones. So many lost years. Instead, she cut to the significant part of the story. "But when Papa developed Alzheimer's, someone had to care for him. My mother was gone by then, and my brother, and I'd bought back the house, so I took him in. And that's when Papa began to explain.

"At first, I thought him delusional." Greta's laugh came out harsh, startling her spaniel. "He *was* delusional, or he never would have spoken of such things. When I asked him, during sentient periods, he denied everything with such vehemence that I stopped asking. But when he confused me with others, with *men* from his past, I became curious and encouraged his stories.

"He admitted to having joined an ancient secret society of powerful men.

"And he admitted to ruining us by crossing them during the War."

Arden had heard much of this story once already. So, while Greta told how her father had challenged the Comitatus and their precious status quo, Arden found herself watching Smith.

Carefully, though, so nobody would notice.

She'd generally avoided him during their youth, despite their fathers' friendship. Smith had been too full of himself, too loud and *boy*like—trouble on two feet. Only when they began moving in the same post-college circles did she really start watching him, still more annoyed than intrigued. His cocky immunity to her charms—and she wasn't foolish enough to deny them—had bothered her. The more caustic the run-ins they had, the more she assumed their dislike to be mutual. They couldn't seem to spend ten minutes in each other's company without finding something to disagree about...which eventually proved downright fascinating. By the time he'd bitten out a sudden invitation to a party, like a dare in the middle of a fight over nothing, she'd been so surprised that she'd stuttered out agreement. And then…

Then the attraction that flared up between them, no longer held back by their pretense of mutual enmity, had almost consumed her.

How long had she already been in love by then?

It wasn't just that he was handsome, though he was. She noted the long line of his back now, the pull of his shoulders under his faded brown T-shirt, worn to a softness she could only imagine under her fingers. She noted the defined muscles of his tanned, bare arms, his elbows on his jeaned knees as he leaned nearer Greta to hear the story. The brush of his too-long brown hair across his neck. That action-hero profile. The stubborn, uncompromising jaw—far more recalcitrant than his daring grins let on—which she could remember kissing the tension out of one night, while his hands had done sinful things across her…

She shifted uncomfortably in the love seat, crossing her ankles, her feet still bare. Smith's gaze slanted momentarily in her direction, dancing with mischief as if he knew just what she'd been remembering, before returning to Greta.

Oh…*sugar.* They should have slept together and gotten it out of their systems, but she was a six-month-minimum girl and they'd kept breaking up at five-and-a-half months, then starting over. Maybe she'd been afraid to surrender that last bit of control, or afraid the reality couldn't match the anticipation, which—good God in heaven! That last time, they were a day from six months and she'd honestly looked forward not just to making love, but to planning a future with him.

And then the phone call.

She should have dated more seriously since their breakup, but none of her gentleman callers had, well…*challenged* her. Not like Smith. Which should have been a good thing, but apparently was not.

He claimed to want to protect her, which shouldn't make her feel quite as gooey inside as it did. The warmth of his body, so close to hers in this un-air-conditioned home, was bad enough without her mistaking stalking for affection. *He'd come back*—which, as far as reasons to like him went, was even worse.

He didn't deserve a second—or was that a fifth?—chance. She couldn't respect herself if she gave him one. Not that he'd even asked. What if he didn't?

Arden felt far more threatened by Smith's return than by any supposed Comitatus.

Val's voice cut through her thoughts. "So you think he told you all these supposed secrets because of the Alzheimer's?"

"I'm sure of it," agreed Greta. "To hear him speak of it, the Comitatus were once a society of honor. A society formed by heroes of history and legend. But he finally faced that they'd lost their way, and he was well rid of them. His only regret, in speaking out against their interests, was how his exile harmed the rest of us."

Again, Arden took the older woman's hand. She could only imagine how similar ruin would pain her own father. "Daddies want to take care of their little girls."

Did she imagine something odd in Greta's expression at that? She must have, because all Greta said was, "My only regret will be if one of you is hurt doing a kindness for an old woman. As you said, Arden—the attack on you last night confirms that my father's story was true. That is enough."

"Enough?" repeated Arden, more unwilling than unable to understand.

"You must leave the matter alone." Greta patted Arden's hand and released it, then petted Dido's head before sitting back. "Let it go, just as you were asked. If you pose no further threat to this society's secrets, they may pose no further threat to you."

"And let them *win?*" Arden looked from Greta's faded,

pleading eyes to Val's pragmatic agreement. "They ruined your family, Greta! And they think they can threaten me with a knife to get their own way? If we let it go, they'll think that's appropriate behavior!"

"Seems like they already believe that," noted Val drily.

"But it isn't!" In desperation, she turned to Smith. Smith was nothing if not a rebel. Surely he would—

But even Smith, she could see by his wince, agreed with the others. Arden felt as betrayed as she had when he'd called to dump her, no explanation offered, the night they would have…

"It's not just that it's dangerous." At least he knew *that* argument didn't stand a chance against her. "But Greta's the one who asked you to look into this, Ard. Now Greta's asking you to stop. How polite is it to ignore her?"

Arden rarely scowled—it encouraged wrinkles—but she felt her eyes narrow at how easily Smith hit her weak spots.

"Greta's not just being nice, *Ard*," insisted Val. "This isn't like, 'You take the last cookie,' 'No, *you* take the last cookie.' We don't want to have to worry about you!"

"Exactly—" Smith cut himself off long enough to exchange a suspicious glance with Val, both surprised to find themselves on the same side of an argument. "Going after the Comitatus won't just draw attention to you. What makes you think it won't draw attention to Greta, as well? Or your rec center? For all you know, someone could have followed you here."

"Obviously," noted Arden, glaring daggers.

"Someone *else*."

"If there's any chance of danger to Greta, then I certainly can't just leave."

"Remember what I used to do for a living?" *Used* to? For the first time, Arden noted how Smith's jeans weren't artfully worn—they were well and truly worn. Gone was his expensive diving watch. His overlong hair couldn't possibly be a fashion statement. Not without any product.

"You worked in security," she admitted softly, trying to grasp the concept. Smith hadn't just left her. He must have left Donnell Security—a business he'd built himself. Smith was…poor.

But he was a Donnell of the Fort Worth Donnells. That simply made no sense.

"If it'll put your mind at ease, I'll set up a security system for Greta," Smith continued. "Will that make everyone happy?"

Val stared at him. "Not me. Why should we trust you?"

But Greta said, "Any friend of Arden's, dear." So that was that.

Then Smith just had to go and smile—no, *smirk*—at Arden, as if he'd won something.

"Friend? We *weren't that close*," she insisted, slipping her feet into her pumps and standing.

If only she could make that true.

Chapter 4

Smith tried not to flinch from Arden's casual dismissal. "Hey now, sweetness—you aren't ashamed of me, are you?"

She arched an accusing eyebrow.

"Oh," he said, not quite as cocky. "You are, huh?"

"As delightful as this has been, what with the history lesson and the stalking, I really do have to go," Arden insisted. Then she actually smiled.

A warm, real smile.

Smith's traitorous heart leaped.

"Jeffie's coming home from camp today," she explained. So the smile was for her half brother, not for Smith. "I'm picking him up at the airpo—"

"Too much information," Smith interrupted. How many times had he warned her that the fastest way to be victimized was to let down one's guard? In light of that, it was probably just as well she *didn't* trust him. Dammit.

Arden waved him away like an annoying bug as, with a quick hug for Greta and pat for Dido, she headed out.

"Too much information?" he heard Val demand as the younger women left, the dog whining from her exile at the door. "It's not like you said you'd been on the toilet all morning or anything."

He had to imagine the expression on Arden's face.

Smith's expression might have rivaled it as he watched the women reach the sidewalk. Greta Kaiser said, "You love her."

It wasn't a question.

Spinning to face the old woman, Smith pretended it had been. "Me? No. Sure, we were dating when…" *When I lost everything she might have wanted from me.* He grinned to reinforce his position. "No love. Maybe some like, if you squint at it and turn your head just right."

Oh, great job. Make sight jokes to a near-blind woman.

"I'll just call a friend of mine to bring over the supplies we need for that security system," he said.

"Help me with these dishes when you've a moment, please?" asked Greta mildly, and vanished into the kitchen.

No, Arden was definitely not the only too-trusting woman involved in this latest problem.

As he sat in his car, waiting for Arden and her "friend" to leave the run-down old house they'd come to visit, Prescott Lowell used his laptop to pull up the area tax records.

The house was owned by someone named Greta Lorelai Kaiser.

It didn't sound familiar, but he made note of it all the same. No surprise that she was a single woman home owner. From what he knew of Donaldson Leigh's stuck-up bitch of a daughter—opening a recreational center especially for girls, supporting a woman for governor—Lowell figured them for feminazis. Throw in the Mexican woman, who'd almost spotted him as he tailed them from the train station, and there was probably enough estrogen in that house to lower a guy's IQ by fifty points.

Not that Lowell didn't like women! But they had their place.

He loved that about the Comitatus. *Everyone* had their place. And the place of Comitatus members was on top of everyone else.

That was the only reason he'd kept himself from fighting back when Leigh had humiliated him last night, when he'd *really* wanted to knock the old geezer's teeth in. There was an *order* to things—at least within the social sanctuary that was the Comitatus. The younger members of the outer circles respected the older members of the inner circles, because someday they would be part of those inner circles themselves. They would run things the *right* way.

With strength.

Leigh and his cronies seemed annoyingly tolerant of the threat posed by Arden's interference. What the hell had Will Donnell meant about womenfolk having suspicions, and "ways to divert them," anyway? If women stuck their noses into men's business, as far as Lowell was concerned, you smacked them back so they wouldn't do it again. *That* was how to divert them.

But there was no reasoning with Leigh about his precious little girl. So it was up to Lowell to uncover the truth for those inner-circle powermongers, and…

Ah. Here came Arden and her brown-skinned friend now. The friend, clearly low-class, scanned the area around them. For a moment, her eyes paused on Lowell's car, well down the street. Seeing nothing more suspicious than a luxury vehicle in a cesspool of a neighborhood, she scowled but moved on. Arden, in contrast, looked deceptively refined in a full-skirted sundress and a large, shady hat. She acted as if she had no need of monitoring her surroundings, she was that confident in her place of the world.

Idiot.

Certain he knew where they were going—public transit, again—Lowell waited until the women had almost reached the end of the block before turning the key in the ignition. It wasn't like they would hear the purr of his finely tuned engine. Shifting into gear, he eased forward....

Tried to ease forward.

A thumping lurch dragged his attention from his quarry to his car. He pressed harder on the gas, forcing the sedan to move, and the thumps sped up.

Braking, Lowell cut the engine and climbed out into the heat to face a flat tire on the driver's side front.

And the driver's side back.

Circling the car, he found the other two tires equally flat. A piece of toothpick, still extending from the valve of one tire, explained how someone had sabotaged the car without him hearing it, or even noticing the slow sinking of the vehicle. Instead of puncturing the tires, someone had arranged for a slow leak in all four.

But—the girls had been in the house the whole time!

Lowell glanced quickly around him, his eyes narrowing at some teenaged boys of mixed ethnicities playing basketball not far down the street. They had worse ways, he supposed, of trapping a fine automobile in this slum, maybe to steal its hubcaps, maybe to do worse.

Narrowing his eyes in warning, Lowell slipped quickly back into the car to phone for auto-club service. But first he pressed the button to lock all his doors and made sure he knew where his gun was, as opposed to his knife.

None of the bloodlines around here deserved an honorable fight!

Grinning from one of Greta's windows at his automotive handiwork, Smith quickly finished dictating which security system to pick up. "No, let's not go with the base level—and yes, I'll pay you back. Let's go for deluxe. If certain parties figure out who she is—"

"Who *is* she?" demanded Trace over the prepaid cell phone.

"I'll explain later. 'Bye." Then, pocketing the phone, Smith carried the last of the dishes into the kitchen after his elderly hostess, careful not to trip on the dog. Living hand-to-mouth as he now did, he'd gotten pretty skilled at bussing tables.

Descended from heroes of history and legend, huh?

Even as he set down the dishes, the older lady asked, "How well did you know Arden *before* you and she began dating?"

"Not that well—"

"I can ask her, too," Greta reminded him, turning the faucet on in her deep old sink. The pipes made a hollow clunk as the water began to run.

"Our families were close, but we didn't see each other much," Smith admitted guiltily. Especially not as he'd entered his rebellious teen years, when he might have found her something other than "icky." Back then, he'd avoided all social obligations like the plague. "Not until after college. I just… That is, she…"

She'd seemed so perfect, he'd thought she would never look twice at him. So he'd pretended disinterest.

Familiarity breeding contempt, she'd met his disinterest and raised him some exasperation.

He'd matched her exasperation and added some scorn. This had gone on for years.

It was Mitch who'd finally called Smith on his behavior. *For two people who can't stand each other, you two sure do end up in the same place a lot.*

Thus began their equally turbulent, on-again off-again attempts at dating without killing each other. He'd never had so much fun. Never felt so much frustration.

Just nail her and get it over with already, Trace had insisted. But Arden had this old-fashioned six-month rule, and they never made it past four without one blowup or another, until finally…

Wait. Why was it any of the old bat's business? "It was complicated."

"You loved her," Greta repeated, adding dish soap.

"No man who loves a woman would dump her, drunk, over the phone."

"Unless he was protecting her." She turned to fix her seemingly sightless eyes on him. "Just as you're trying to protect her now."

Smith stared back. Silence seemed his best option here.

"You were well-off and respected. Suddenly you had nothing. Meant nothing—at least to the world the pair of you knew. My father's story must sound familiar."

This was getting uncomfortable. "So why don't I do a walk-through of the house, start prepping for when Trace gets here with the security equipment?"

"Quite the dilemma," murmured Greta. "You took a vow of honor not to speak of it, yet your own honesty won't let you deny it. Don't worry. That's all the proof I need or will ask of you.

"You are Comitatus. Of the blood. Of the tradition. This is how you know exactly what dangers Arden faces. And you, Smith Donnell, were exiled—just like my father."

Smith opened his mouth to protest—he could so be dishonest! But Greta silenced him with a raised, gnarled hand. "This is why I believe you should have this."

"Have…?"

She stooped, pressed on a piece of the built-in shelving—and a panel suddenly swung loose from the wall.

She had an honest-to-God hidden compartment.

No wonder she'd bought the house back!

Smith watched as she swung the panel back on a hidden hinge and claimed a slim, velvet-wrapped bundle, not a yard long. She laid her treasure on the kitchen table and slowly, reverently, folded back its rich purple wrapping to reveal—

Smith stared.

It was a sword. A double-edged short sword, to be precise, and yet, somehow…more. It caught the summer shadows as if it glowed.

But swords didn't glow. Especially not seriously old swords—and this one was *seriously* old…or, more likely, a replica. It looked like something from some gladiator movie, *Troy* or *Spartacus*. The blade, extending out of a hilt studded with green gemstones, expanded into a swell at the tip that gave the oddly gold-colored metal a faint leaf-shape.

An impression of sand and salty wind swirled into Smith's mind for just a moment before he blinked it away.

"The sword of Aeneas," Greta explained softly.

Smith stared at the sword. Then at the old woman he'd just met. Then back down at the sword.

Well, that was unexpected.

"The what of which?"

"Woo hoo!" exclaimed fourteen-year-old Jefferson Leigh, sliding his leather backpack across the front foyer like a bowling ball. "I'm *home!*"

"Yes, you are," agreed Arden as she closed the door behind him, taking pleasure from her baby brother's high spirits. She'd needed a distraction from the return of Smith Donnell into her life, and Jeff, as always, did the job. His cheeks glowed with health under dark hair even curlier than hers. Camp in Switzerland had energized him. "Which is why we do not throw luggage."

"*Ar*den!"

"*Jef*fie!" she parroted back his long-suffering moan, eliciting another grin. "Carry your bag to your room and I'll make sure Esperanza has a snack for us, all right?"

He saluted. "Ma'am, yes, ma'am!" As if it had been some kind of military camp, instead of a training ground for sons of privilege.

She couldn't believe how he'd grown in two short months, all feet and elbows. Then their father came in from the backyard—from his detached office—and she believed it after all. Donaldson Leigh was no small man, himself.

"Jeff!" he bellowed. "Let the help take care of your bags and come tell me about camp! Arden, you're staying the night to spend time with your brother, aren't you?"

When Jeff turned his big eyes on her, Arden was lost. Heaven knew she could ignore Smith's warnings of possible danger to *her*. She could even dismiss Val and Greta's concern as paranoia. She could resist her father's paternal pushiness. But Jeffie…?

And what could be safer than her father's house?

"Of course I am. Go on to the kitchen, I'll meet you there." She watched her father sling a burly arm over Jeff's narrow shoulders, too pleased to force the issue of the backpack. Instead, after they'd vanished, she grabbed the pack and carried it upstairs herself.

She saw no reason why perfectly healthy boys should abandon even their carry-ons. But her stepmother, Jeff's mom, hadn't been gone for a year yet.

Today, it was enough to see her brother smile.

Some men, at least, didn't hide secrets behind every jibe and grin. *Some* men…

But she'd meant to forget Smith. *Sugar.*

Leaving Jeff's backpack on his bed, she felt the unlikely roughness of its leather straps as it slid from her palm. Intrigued, she looked closer.

The good quality of the leather had been nicked and carved, as if by a boy playing with a knife.

Jeff hadn't etched anything disturbing, really—his name, a

frowning face, the symbol of his favorite band. Still, the idea of her baby brother playing with even a Swiss Army knife disturbed her, and not just because of the memory of last night's blade.

Arden reminded herself that she had to let him grow up sometime. He'd turn fifteen in a few weeks. In a year, he would have a learner's permit....

Arden trailed her fingers across the nicked leather—a perfectly good backpack, mutilated—then curled them into a fist. *No.* Not her business.

Wondering why she had such trouble understanding males in general, Arden left Jeff's room and shut the door.

Chapter 5

Long explanations later, Smith still felt lost. Trace would arrive soon with the alarm supplies, probably with Mitch driving. And Smith didn't want that extra complication just yet.

"Wait, wait," he protested as Greta drew breath for yet another recitation. "How about I tell it, and you just see if I've got it right?"

The older woman sat neatly back in her kitchen chair, clasped her frail hands and waited. The sword lay on the table between them, the odd, not-quite-glowing patina of its blade tempting him to touch it.

It tempted him enough to make him seriously wary of it, of anything he could want that badly.

"This warrior, Aeneas. He's the guy from the Roman epic I slogged through in World Lit."

"Virgil's *Aeneid*," she clarified, as if he hadn't actually passed the class.

"You're saying this guy was real."

She smiled, looking not at all insane. "Yes."

"Wasn't his mother a goddess?"

"Much of his story was probably mythologized."

"You don't say." Okay, so that was rude. But Greta *was* apparently crazy. Fair trade.

"Historical details in the story also confuse the timing. Aeneas couldn't have left Troy after its walls fell and still founded Lavinium—Rome—within the same generation. And while Dido of Carthage did exist—"

The dog Dido scampered to her feet, sure they meant her.

"The queen that Aeneas dumped," Smith clarified. "The one who killed herself."

"Yes, the true Dido was a Phoenician exile. However, had she met Aeneas before he founded Rome, he would have been centuries old."

"That's some age difference." Smith took a deep breath. "So, not really from Troy. Not really Dido's lover. And this sword probably wasn't forged by the blacksmith god Vulcan—"

"Greek name Hephaestus."

"—for the invincible warrior Achilles."

Greta smiled a small, mysterious smile, kind of like the one Smith used to see on Arden. He hated—well, loved—no, *hated* that wise, womanly smile. "I like to think it could somehow be true," she said, "but external logic would imply not."

"But this *is* his sword." Ancient. Precious.

Amazingly powerful.

He fisted his hand, resisting the urge to slide a finger down its fuller, the groove that divided the flat of the blade. *Don't touch it. If you do, you'll be lost....*

"So says my family legend."

Smith's own family hadn't been that big on legends. Sure, they traced back to investors of the Peters Colony, some of the earliest white settlers of central Texas. Before that, they went all the way to Jamestown.

But *Troy?* Not so much.

"Your family the Hapsburgs. Of the Holy Roman Empire Hapsburgs. Aren't some of them still running around, heading the family in Austria?"

Dido flopped back onto her tummy, watching them through spaniel eyes.

"In the seventeenth and eighteenth centuries, many of the royal families of Europe experienced schisms, even complete exile, as did the Stuarts of England. The Stuarts who even now head the Comitatus, yes?"

Yes. Last time Smith had checked, two different cousins were vying for the leadership of the society he'd left. Both were named Stuart. "The Comitatus who exiled your father."

"And you," Greta said.

Smith lifted his eyebrows, not about to confirm that. He might resent the society enough to plot their downfall, but he'd also given his vow, at age fifteen, not to share secrets with outsiders.

Something about that age—fifteen—brushed and then vanished from his thoughts. That part didn't matter. What mattered was that keeping those vows was more about *him* than about *them*. It had to be. Even if Greta did have Comitatus blood, she was also a woman.

Hey, *he* hadn't made the rules. And few fifteen-year-old boys see the downside of a guys-only society.

Still, Greta stayed true to her word. She didn't force him to confirm her spot-on suspicions. "The society began to lose its way centuries ago, sometime after the American Revolution. With the loss of monarchies came the loss of noblesse oblige, the understanding that privilege requires responsibility. My father, to judge by his ramblings, left the Comitatus to protest putting Americans into detainment camps. The Japanese weren't the only ones to be detained, you know. Italians and some German-Americans experienced similar atrocities."

She'd said something like that before.

"German-Americans like your father," guessed Smith.

"Papa was not arrested. A Kaiser, descended from the Hapsburgs? Never. But he insisted on defending those without the voice to defend themselves. To hear him speak of it, the Comitatus was once a society of honor. A society formed by heroes like Aeneas. When they began to lose their way, Papa felt they no longer deserved the sword of a hero, and he hid this away.

"Do you think, Smith Donnell, that you may have use of it?"

Smith had been studying the sword through much of this, half convinced that the damned thing was humming to him. His palm ached to grasp the jeweled hilt. How much would it weigh? Could its leaf-shaped blade still hold an edge after all these years?

What was he thinking? "This can't be two-thousand years old and change," he protested, about both the sword and the corrupt society he, too, had escaped. "It would have shattered by now. Wouldn't it?"

"Not if it really was forged by Hephaestus for Achilles."

Smith grinned. "Didn't you say the mythic parts were…mythologized?"

"I said they may have been." Again, her knowing smile reminded him way too much of Arden. Why did the thought of Arden suddenly worry him? "The sword, from wherever it came, is clearly a real weapon."

It was that. Solid. True. But not two- or three-thousand years old, and not *his*. Not before, and certainly not now. Not when—

"Jeff." That's when he remembered, stood. *Hell.*

Greta raised a curious eyebrow.

"Arden's little brother, Jeff. How old is he?" Fifteen, right? Or coming on fifteen? The point of no return?

This clearly wasn't what she'd expected from her presentation of the priceless relic. "Smith, this sword is a legacy. I have no children. My father had no male heirs. I offer you—"

"Yeah, you offer me the Sword of Aeneas. Which is really generous. And, considering that you've known me for an hour since I broke into your house, more than a little disturbing. I'm sorry, Miz Greta. I can't accept it."

She settled back, seemingly more intrigued than disappointed. Dido the dog looked from her to him and back, her silky ears perked.

If he'd had more time, Smith wouldn't have rushed this part. "You don't know me, and I don't know you. I'm not Comitatus—" for more than a year, he hadn't been "—so if you think this sword's going to somehow redeem their honor, it's not for me. I doubt it's really as old as you think. I seriously doubt it belonged to Aeneas, Achilles or Hephaestus. But if it did, I'm definitely not the man for it. I don't *want* it. And—"

A familiar pounding on the front door made Greta jump, but not Smith. He'd learned long ago that Trace couldn't help the power he put behind the most mundane activities.

"If you don't want to advertise this, I suggest you put it back before I introduce you to my friend and business associate," Smith finished over the frantic barking of Dido as she scampered toward the sound of the intruder.

"Then you won't tell anyone that I have it?" Greta watched him very closely, for someone who couldn't see.

More pounding at the door. The dog's barks grew hysterical.

Smith bit back a bitter laugh. "I'm good with secrets."

As he strode toward the front of the house to greet Trace and maybe Mitch, he thought he heard Greta murmur something that didn't really make sense, especially over the noise.

She said, "That's once."

Stepping out of her Italian marble bathroom, back into her bedroom suite, Arden took a grateful draw of cool air. She'd enjoyed their family dinner at the Nasher Sculpture Gardens, especially watching Jeff interact with his favorite oversized pieces in the carefully designed landscape. She'd picked up some literature and numbers, hoping to arrange a field trip for her girls from the rec center someday soon. But the heat of August had come close to disproving the old saying that horses sweat, men perspire, yet women only glow.

When even a lukewarm shower felt cloying and humid, Arden preferred dressing in her room, where billows of steam vanished to nothingness against the powerful air-conditioning. Tucking a fluffy white towel more tightly around her, she padded across the thick carpet to her walk-in closet.

The full-length mirror on the door that she swung open revealed someone sprawled comfortably beneath the arched iron canopy of her filigree bed, arms folded, eyes smoldering sleepily.

She spun with a gasp, only belatedly recognizing Smith.

He yawned. "Hey, Arden. You're back."

"What—?" But her temper tightened her throat beyond the ability to form words. Instead, she reached into her closet, pulled a dress shoe off the shelf and hurled it at him.

It felt good.

He dodged—so much for his comfy sprawl—and even had the nerve to look wounded. "Hey!"

Encouraged by how good that had felt, Arden sent the shoe's mate soaring in his direction, then grabbed another pair.

"Wait!" Smith rolled off the bed, taking partial shelter behind her damask duvet cover. "This isn't how a lady—"

Arden was grabbing shoes with her left hand, throwing them with her right. "A *lady?*"

Was *that* why he'd wanted to hurt her? Because she'd waited before they'd gotten intimate? Because she'd made him prove himself to her? Didn't he realize how agonizing *she'd* found the wait?

"You're not denying it *now,* are—" A calfskin boot bounced off his shoulder. "Ow!"

"A lady wouldn't put up with being dishonored the way

you've been dishonoring me." She hurled a pink-and-white running shoe at him, disappointed by how harmlessly it bounced off her coverlet.

"Dishonored?" He tried to circle around the bed, but ducked back behind an iron post to deflect more missiles. "How many shoes do you have?"

"I'm a Dallas socialite, I've got *plenty!*" She turned to the high heels.

"When have I dishonored you?"

"Breaking into my bedroom, for one! Not telling me you were here. A minute longer, and I might have—" She saw his intense interest in the very idea that she would have dropped the towel in front of him. She rewarded it with a three-inch-heeled strappy number.

"I said hello!"

"And following me to Greta's."

"Hey, Greta *loved* me."

"And showing up last night at my party, a serious function for an important cause the likes of which you would never understand. And asking me to lie to Daddy for you!"

"Did I thank you for that?" His words came from beyond the bed, where he'd crouched pretty low to avoid the worst of her shoes.

The *you're welcome* that crowded into Arden's throat, a social training she could hardly deny even in the midst of her fury, made her laugh bitterly. Then, dropping the shoes she held, she heard her laugh twist into something more like a sob. Oh…*sugar.*

Smith reappeared beyond the bed. "Ard?"

She hid her face in her hands. "Don't call me that."

"Is it safe to come out?"

She nodded, keeping an eye on him through her fingers. But then, as he rose to his full height—so concerned, so lean, so Smith—she reconsidered and moved her hands. *"You dumped me!"*

To her surprise, he didn't duck again. He just stood there, exposed to whatever she wanted to throw at him, and stared at her with something that could almost be…regret.

"Yeah," he admitted, finally. "I did."

Don't make me ask you. Please don't make me ask you. She tried to express the plea with her eyes, unwilling to lower herself further. No matter what they'd been—and *almost* been—to each other, he didn't deserve her time, much less her deference.

Maybe he understood, at that. "I wish I could explain why." His expression, steady and solemn, actually matched his words. "God, you can't know how much I've wanted to."

"So, *do.*" True, she wore only a towel—two towels, if you counted the one wrapping her newly washed hair. But she could still bring on the poise if she had to. She could still bring on the air of entitlement.

"I can't."

"Why not?"

"Because I made a promise. I—" Reading something in her expression, he interrupted himself and her reaction. "Here's what I *can* tell you. Will you let me do that much?"

The moment stretched between them. Then, bolstered by the promise of finally knowing something, anything—and maybe, unhealthily, by the promise of a little more time in Smith's long-lost presence—Arden nodded. "Wait here while I get dressed."

"Do you have to?"

She threw another shoe at him—a halfhearted toss that he easily dodged—before stepping into her spacious closet and closing the door behind her. The temptation to dress for him, to put on a nice frock or, worse, a slinky nightgown, sped her pulse. She resisted it. Instead, she slipped into a sleeveless T-shirt and some pink boxer shorts before toweling her hair off one last time and heading back out.

Hair uncombed. No makeup. No jewelry. How better to send the message that she wanted no more to do with him after their talk.

Other than calling for Daddy to throw him out, anyway.

So why, turning back from her cold fireplace, did he stare at her as if she'd dressed for a date? Even now, a year after his betrayal, her stomach shivered at the brush of Smith's gaze, at her power to momentarily silence him.

"Please, have a seat." She sank into one of two bergère armchairs arranged in front of the fireplace, as polite as seemed wise, considering. "I would offer you refreshments, but…"

"The kitchen's closed?" he suggested, eyes dancing.

"You broke in," she corrected smoothly.

"Nothing's broken, honestly."

"Smith."

He took the chair opposite her. "Okay. Why I, er, ended our relationship."

She waited.

"I didn't want to," he offered weakly.

She rolled her eyes—only he could prompt so rude a gesture. "Please. When's the last time you did *anything* you didn't want to do?"

"All the time, lately! I didn't want to give up my business. I sure don't want to be living off the grid. And losing you—" Mouth tight, he shook his head. "I did it. I'm not denying that. In the same circumstances, I would again. But Arden…" Smith sat forward in his seat, leaned nearer to her. "It's the hardest thing I've ever done, leaving you. That's why I had to get drunk to do it. It'll probably go down as the biggest regret of my life. You deserve to know that much."

The words of a con man. Except…

He'd never been able to con her. Nor she, him. Their truths somehow linked them, even in their worst fights. Even now.

Only as she felt her shoulders imperceptibly relax did

Arden realize just how much she'd longed to hear similar words. *He hadn't wanted to do it. He regretted it, too.* She had to remind herself that neither point made anything better. "So why *did* you?"

"I…" His gaze skimmed across the marble floor as if looking for the exact right balance between what he supposedly could and could not tell her. "I made some enemies."

"You? No!"

His lips pulled into a reluctant smile. "It's true. I had a…disagreement. With some of my associates. They had more clout than I did, and I lost. I mean—I had a choice. Give in to them, or lose everything. I made my choice."

Arden scowled. "So this was some stupid matter of pride?"

"It was a matter of honor." Smith scowled harder.

"How?"

"I…" He sat back, crossed his arms and his booted feet, wouldn't meet her gaze. "I can't tell you that part."

And to think she'd almost begun to forgive him! Arden rose to her bare feet, backed away from him and everything he'd once meant to her, everything he'd so easily discarded. "How very convenient for you."

"Convenient?" Smith stood, as well. "Hell, Arden, tell me one convenient thing about this! I lost my business. I lost my money. I was all but disowned by my family. Worst of all, I lost *you.*"

She stared at him, here in her bedroom, a strange amalgam of the man she'd thought she'd loved and a complete stranger.

When he took a step toward her, then another, she refused to back away.

"I lost *you,*" he repeated more softly, and now he stood only a step away from her. Now he stood right in front of her; she could smell the dry heat of the day's sweat—perspiration— and something else hot, like coals, like fire. Now he'd lifted a hand, warm and dry, to her cool shoulder. "None of this was your fault, and I hurt you anyway, and I'm sorry. I'm so very, very sorry."

Sorry. The word that she'd apparently longed for the most.

She wasn't ready to forgive him. And she certainly wasn't ready to kiss him. But the apology soothed something deep inside her, something that had been raw and festering for over a year, and—foolish and weak or not—she couldn't just ignore that. So she leaned across those last inches of space between them, leaned into the tall, hard strength of him. She tucked her head down, rested her cheek on the soft, worn cotton of his T-shirted shoulder.

And when his arms lifted tentatively around her, then drew her more firmly against him, she sighed out more pain than she'd realized she'd held on to.

Their truths. Linked.

It didn't fix anything, of course. But it was something.

For the moment, it was enough.

Chapter 6

Arden seemed deceptively frail in Smith's arms, her skin still moist from her shower, her thick black hair damp and tangled under his chin. Did she have any idea how much he loved seeing her so bare of the mask of her makeup, her fine clothes and jewels, her styled hair? It had happened so rarely in their time together—a day at the beach, an evening caught in the rain. He'd longed to someday see her like that in his bed, waking up after a night of lovemaking, but first her damned rules and then the Comitatus had gotten in the way of those hopes. Now she looked as real and vulnerable as he'd imagined. Someone he really could have had as his own. And so very, very hard to consider ever leaving again.

Not that he had any invitation to stay.

Not that he could accept, if she extended one. And yet...

"I've missed you," he admitted softly, wishing his words didn't sound so thick with emotion.

She sighed again, into his collarbone, and Smith tried to

remember why he'd come to see her. He tried to remember why he'd decided to wait here, after checking her condo and then slipping into her father's empty home. He'd wanted to ask something…to ask…

But hell. He'd never been that honorable.

His face burrowed into her jetty, damp curls. He breathed in the sweet scent of her—magnolias and shampoo and woman—until his lips found the bare column of her neck, between her throat and her nape, and he had to taste her, to drink her.

She moaned quietly, drawing her spread hands slowly up his chest and toward his shoulders. He continued kissing her jaw, tasting her ear, and groaned his own contentment as she wove her fingers into his hair, guided his head as she tipped her face toward his.

He first noticed the smudges as he bent to meet her lips with his own.

He ignored it. Nowhere *near* that honorable.

He claimed her as he'd hesitated to do for too long, too long ago. And the kiss was perfect. Right. At first their lips teased across each other's, an echo of the game that they'd played together so often. Then, in another honest echo, they lost control of any games and opened to each other, parted their lips, opened their souls. Their tongues didn't spar, they caressed. The taste of her, oh, Lord, the taste…

He tipped his forehead against hers only to catch a breath, only to admire the naked pleasure in her thick-lashed, deep green eyes. But then he saw the smudges again, across the otherwise clean, creamy perfection of her heart-shaped face. Nothing so dramatic as coal, or soot. But something had bruised or dirtied her, nevertheless…

His confusion didn't last long enough.

It was him.

He hadn't washed up after installing Greta's new security

system. He'd worn the same old T-shirt, the same jeans, heedless of their dusty afternoon job. Now he'd dirtied her with it.

Even he couldn't miss the symbolism.

Arden made an impatient, kittenish noise and stretched upward for his lips. Not being an idiot, he gave them. So sweet. Such treasure.

But not for him.

He ignored the inner protest, bent even closer against her, embracing her in his filthy arms as he kissed the living sin out of her.

And kissed her. And kissed her. Exiled no more.

Until something—a door, a floorboard, a window—creaked.

Smith jumped, overly alert from his months of living underground, and the moment ended. After a quick glance around them, noting the complete lack of danger—*old houses settle, idiot*—Smith's gaze returned to Arden's in time to watch the moment ending in her eyes. They'd focused from hazy wonder into slow realization, and now they narrowed into annoyance.

Probably at herself as much as him. But it was probably better for her if he took her share of that, too. So he deliberately grinned, devil-may-care, as he said, "Sorry 'bout the dirt."

Her cute nose wrinkled in confusion before she followed his dipped gaze to see the smears of dust across her creamy arms, her once-clean shirt.

He expected anger. *Deserved* anger. Her anger would free him to get back to doing what he had to do: destroy the Comitatus, even her father.

Even his.

He didn't realize just how desperately he needed the release of her fury until he didn't get it. Instead, Arden Leigh smiled her beauty-queen smile, poised and artificial as manufactured sweetener.

"Don't you fret yourself about it," she purred. "It's nothing a little soap and water can't fix."

The contrast between this controlled, public Arden and the *real* Arden he'd just been kissing stabbed through Smith's gut. That had to be why he taunted her, grinning more widely. "Well, hell, sweetness. If you like it dirty…"

All he got was a flash, a bare moment of green-eyed annoyance, before her laugh usurped it. "Now you behave yourself, Smith Donnell, or I'll have to call my Daddy on you."

They locked gazes, her smile as grim as his glare felt desperate.

She didn't know how badly it would endanger him—maybe both of them—to be found together. This would be no casual trespass between acquaintances to her Comitatus father.

This would be treason.

Arden could never know that, though, not even if Smith longed to forget it. He'd taken a stupid damned vow.

If he destroyed the Comitatus, would it still matter?

But he couldn't destroy her father without destroying her, could he?

Hell. At least her society-girl mask made that thought a little easier. Just not a lot.

He'd come here for something, hadn't he?

"How's your brother doing?" Smith asked, relieved to see her lovely mask crumble, unexpectedly, behind honest and protective fury.

"Jeff is none of your business!"

"Whoa—I didn't say he was. Just being sociable," he lied. Through his teeth. "How old is he now? Thirteen?"

"Almost fifteen." But she withheld more details.

To ask *really? when?* would further rouse her suspicions. But with a big Comitatus meeting coming up, what better time to swear the boy into his ancestral obligations? And once Jeff had taken vows to the organization, he would be trapped, just as Smith, Mitch and Trace had been trapped.

"Have you considered taking a long vacation with him? You can get some really affordable last-minute deals overseas…" Right. Like she needed affordable.

"You need to go now," declared Arden, since Smith wasn't taking his social cue. "Whatever you came for, you can ask me tomorrow. *Somewhere else.*"

Smith remembered Jeff, an open, idealistic, curly haired kid. Someone who could do some *good* in the world, if he wasn't hijacked to the dark side first.

Smith had liked him.

He also liked how Arden dropped her pretenses when things concerned Jeff. She'd all but herded him out the door onto her balcony, overlooking the back gardens, before he realized what she was doing.

He liked that side of her a lot.

"Oh, that," he agreed, pausing for the afterthought as if that, and not Jeff, had been his excuse for coming here. "Tomorrow. I'd like you to set up a meeting with this Vox07 person, the conspiracy buff who offered to trade information—"

"Tomorrow," she insisted, outright cutting him off. Goodbye, southern belle. Hello, lover.

"Shall I pick you up here?" He wouldn't dare; he just wanted to keep her riled. To spend a few more minutes with her in this mood.

"No. Come by the rec center."

"Isn't that for girls?"

She planted both hands on his chest and pushed. "We don't have cooties."

"If you insist." Now he was just being ornery…but it was so fun!

"I do."

"Because—"

"Smith!" She leveled her dark green gaze at him. "Get *out.*"

Grinning and feeling as if he'd won some kind of contest, Smith slipped out onto her dark balcony, jumped to the lawn and headed back toward his crappy, pay-by-the-week apartment.

The next morning, at breakfast, Jeff looked up from his egg cup and asked, "Whatever happened to that guy you used to date? The sarcastic one?"

Arden's surprisingly sunny mood stuttered to a halt. *What did he know?* "Smith?"

"Uh-huh." Jeff's dark eyes seemed innocent enough, but…could she ever see her brother as anything else? Even a few weeks short of fifteen, he would always be a baby to her.

Their father's gaze held a lot more weight. "Donnell and Arden parted ways over a year ago. Isn't that right, bunny?"

"Yes, Daddy." She felt as if she were lying. But she *wasn't*…except by omission. Just because she'd seen Smith. And lied about it. And kissed him. And dreamed about him….

But that had been Smith's fault. And they certainly weren't dating anymore!

"Good riddance." Her father patted her shoulder affectionately. "You can do much better than that one."

Arden almost didn't challenge that. She didn't care enough about Smith for it to matter, and why disturb their pleasant family morning? But maybe last night's sparring—or the kissing—had left her more quarrelsome than usual. She paused only long enough to dimple a smile at her father and take a sip of fresh orange juice before she asked, "Why is that, Daddy?"

Donaldson Leigh blinked. "Pardon?"

"Why are you so sure Smith was beneath me?"

His own smile brightened the already sunny breakfast nook in what he clearly thought was understanding. "Because, my darling, all men are beneath you. You outshine every last sorry one of them."

Which was characteristically sweet of him, and gratifying

to hear, and yet…"So you didn't have a problem with Smith himself, then?" At his raised eyebrows, Arden wrinkled her nose to imply she was teasing. "I would hate you to think your only daughter had been slumming."

"Not at all!"

Good, she thought.

"Will Donnell is a good friend of mine," her father assured her. "He and his wife were at your soiree just the other night, weren't they?"

Arden felt even more reassured, until he added, "Too bad that boy of his didn't live up to the family name."

Did Daddy know more about Smith's fall from society than she'd thought? Pride had kept her from discussing Smith with him, afterward, and certainly with his parents. But she'd rather disposed of pride last night, in Smith's arms, hadn't she?

Until you kicked him out. She'd had enough pride for that.

Fully aware of Jeff watching the exchange too closely, Arden said, "You know, I never did understand what happened to Smith after our breakup. One week he was running a security company, the next he not only left me, but vanished out of our circle entirely. His mother didn't even mention him to me at the Molly for Governor reception."

Her father took a long sip of coffee.

Her suspicions flared. "Daddy—you didn't do something to Smith, did you? I mean, to protect my honor or something?"

Her father laughed at the foolishness of her question.

So why had he seemed so startled a moment beforehand?

She was drawing breath to ask when Jeff, reaching for the salt, knocked her half-full juice glass over onto the white tablecloth.

He blinked at the mess. "Oops."

Arden leaped to her feet and began attacking the stain with napkins. Their father called for the maid. And in the temporary chaos, the moment passed. Before Arden could decide how to best approach the question, Jeff was asking to come to work with her.

"I want to see what you've done with the place," he insisted. "Especially since that state comptroller lady got involved. I bet you've gotten all kinds of donations."

First questions about Smith, and now the rec center—where she would be meeting Smith today? If Jeff hadn't overheard something, the coincidence amazed her…too much. She stayed suspicious.

"And I can help protect you," Jeff insisted. "Dad always worries about you down in Oak Cliff alone."

"That's true," their father agreed.

Arden quickly prioritized her concerns. "I wish you two would stop acting as if Oak Cliff were the Gaza Strip. It's a perfectly nice neighborhood—"

"Except for when your car radio was stolen," her father reminded her grimly.

"Well, yes, but—"

"Twice."

"We have better security on our parking lot now. Do you think the girls who come to us don't have big brothers and fathers or boyfriends making sure that nobody messes with us?" Well—nobody except the occasionally abusive big brother or father or boyfriend. But Val handled problems like that very well. Speaking of which… "And mothers," she added belatedly. "And sisters."

"Fine! Excuse me for wanting to spend time with my big sister." Jeff slumped dramatically back in his chair as Esperanza cleared the last of the orange-juice detritus. He folded his lanky arms, stared at the ceiling. "I try to show some interest in the things that matter to her, but does she care?"

Despite other concerns, Arden exchanged a glance of amused exasperation with their father. "How about you show some interest tomorrow," she suggested. "Mondays are a little chaotic for bringing visitors."

Whatever he knew, this would be the test.

To her sincere relief, Jeff passed. "Sure. Warn everyone so they can hide your girly secrets away."

"Thank you for enabling us." She bent to kiss his cheek and had to lean extra far as he pulled a face and dodged the embrace. But he couldn't have been trying too hard. He was surprisingly strong lately, but still got kissed.

"You'll be careful," warned her father, happy to offer *his* cheek for a kiss.

"I am always careful." Arden sighed.

Despite that I'm investigating a secret society.

Despite that I'm meeting with Smith Donnell in secret.

And despite that I'm kind of looking forward to it.

That could be the most dangerous part of all.

Jeff was thundering down the stairs later that morning when, at the widening base of them, a heavy hand caught his arm and swung him to a stop.

His father wasted no time getting to the point. "Why were you asking your sister about Smith Donnell at breakfast?"

Because he snuck into her room last night. But Jeff hesitated to tattle, loyalties divided. He loved his father and Arden equally. At camp this summer, he'd heard rumors that maybe he was part of the special bloodline that had created a secret society that would rule the world—he was jazzed to confirm that with Dad! And he was pretty ticked off at Arden about giving Smith the time of day after the way he'd treated her. But...

Well, since his mom had died, Arden had been trying to fill the role of mother and sister combined. She'd never treated him like just a half brother. The sibling bond of secrecy had to be strong for any family to survive.

Anyway, no one liked a tattletale.

So Jeff just shrugged—for now. "No reason."

His dad gave him the evil eye, so Jeff laughed and lied flat out. "Some guys at camp were talking about their big sisters getting married. I wanted to make sure we weren't gonna be dealing with a bridezilla anytime soon."

It worked. His father grinned at the face of disgust Jeff pulled. "So glad to hear you have your sister's well-being in mind," he said drily.

"That's our job," said Jeff—dead serious, this time. Protecting Arden from Oak Cliff ruffians and loser ex-boyfriends alike. Being heroes. "Right?"

And his dad said, "Right."

Before Greta could offer Smith the Sword of Aeneas for a second time, Smith had worked up one hell of a bad mood. Neither Mitch nor Trace showed up at their rat-hole of an apartment. They weren't answering their disposable cell phones either, which had him worrying for his friends' safety. This latest infiltration of the Comitatus through Donaldson Leigh's meeting, to learn and usurp their plans, had mainly been his idea.

Smith hated guilt.

Worse, he'd left Arden. Again. That kiss, a bare taste of what he'd lost, hadn't satisfied him for as long as he might have hoped. His mood wasn't improved by the thought that it would have to last him forever.

All that, and he'd slept badly, dreaming of wooden ships and ancient warriors, of love versus duty.

Of making the wrong choice.

Again.

At least he would see Arden again today. The first thing he did after waking up alone—still no sign of Trace or Mitch—was to go by the coin-operated Laundromat to make sure that this time, he could at least be clean. Not that he expected another chance to take her in his arms and kiss her.

Laundromats rarely improved his mood, either.

Only when he caught a light-rail south to the Westmoreland station, and stopped by Greta's to see how the security had held, did things click into place. Mitch's latest fixer-upper of a car drooped tiredly in the yard. Although Mitch often drove a cab to earn extra money, he had to do it illegally, borrowing the taxi and permit. The rest of the time, he practiced his mechanical skills on downright embarrassing vehicles—which at least ran.

Greta didn't answer the door.

Trace—and the cocker spaniel—did.

Trace was eating a cinnamon bun.

"Hey," the larger man greeted, swinging the door open wider as if welcoming Smith to *his* abode, and not Miz Kaiser's. "She made breakfast."

Smith stared. "What are you doing up and out before noon?" Trace often did construction when he was home in Louisiana, but while he was in Texas, he mainly focused on fighting. For money. It was a nighttime activity.

"Up." Trace licked a bit of frosting off his big thumb. "Not out."

Automatically crouching to scratch the welcoming, wiggling Dido behind her silky ears, Smith took in Trace's bare feet. *"You spent the night?"*

"She offered! She's got all kinds of spare room." Apparently sensing Smith's annoyance, Trace grumped, "Mitch stayed over, too."

"I asked you guys to finish the security system, not to crash here!"

In answer, Trace popped the last of the bun into his mouth, folded his arms, spread his stance—and blocked the doorway more effectively than any security bars could have.

Smith had to grant him that one. "Breakfast, huh?"

Trace grunted but pivoted out of the way, and Smith headed back toward the kitchen with his four-legged shadow. He tried not to glance toward the panel that hid the Sword of Aeneas.

He failed. Was the wall *humming,* or was it…?

Just him.

Mitch, equally disheveled, bent to pet the returning Dido while he grinned up at something Greta had told him. "So you just *flashed* him?"

"I was wearing undergarments," Greta clarified primly.

Smith wasn't sure he wanted to hear this, but a laughing Mitch had caught sight of him in the hallway. "Hey, Smith! Back when women were still supposed to just wear skirts, some jerk told Greta she must be a guy for wearing pants, and she flashed him to prove him wrong! How great is she?"

Trace, following Smith into the old-fashioned kitchen, perked up. "Someone flashed someone?"

"Greta," Mitch agreed, then hooted at the face Trace pulled.

"Unless I'm looking straight at you, I can still see you," chided Greta gently, even as she poured a cup of coffee and turned to hand it to Smith.

"No offense." But Trace's expression didn't vanish as he dropped comfortably into a chair.

"Ah." Smith took the coffee with a murmur of thanks and inhaled deeply before taking a sip. "To be forty years older. Really," he insisted when Greta waved the seeming compliment away. "The way things have been going this last year, I'm not especially confident about making it five years more, much less forty. So what's this about my employees taking advantage of your kind hospitality, Miz Greta?"

Trace snorted. "Employees?"

"That term," Mitch explained, as Smith took another swallow of good, hot coffee, "implies some form of wages. From you. To us."

"I invited them," Greta insisted. "First for dinner, if Mitch would give me a ride to the market—it was the least I could do, after all that work you boys did on the security system. Then it seemed such a shame to send them out, once night had come."

"Them being scared of the dark and all." Smith arched a challenging brow at Trace.

"I haven't slept so well for years." Settling herself into a third kitchen chair, Greta opened her hand for Dido's affectionate head. "Having a dog in the house is all well and good, but strong young men…"

"That—" Trace squared his broad shoulders "—would be us."

Smith rolled his eyes over his coffee cup. "I didn't imagine she was talking about the security elves."

"And, the place doesn't smell like feet," noted Mitch, his blue eyes half closed in apparent bliss. "Did you ever notice how all our cruddy hotel rooms smell like feet? Maybe Greta would be willing to consider some kind of barter deal."

"No. No barter deals. No settling in for coffee and home-cooked dinners and cinnamon—" Smith finally took in the sticky, empty platter in the middle of Greta's table. "There aren't any cinnamon buns left?"

"Didn't know you were coming." Trace licked his fingers again, adding insult to injury. Dido licked her lips.

"That's because neither of you answered your phones!"

His friends exchanged looks that went from confusion to realization. "We silenced them during the movie," Mitch explained. "After I got Greta's VCR to work with her new large button remote control. She's got some real classics on tape, and as long as we were here—"

"Never mind. Greta, could I see you in the front room?" Smith left the mug on the counter as he followed the older woman—and her dog—toward the parlor. At least from there he couldn't keep stealing glances toward the hidden panel. "You can't let them take advantage of you."

"Shame on you!" Well—that surprised him. He hadn't expected the old lady to go on the offensive quite this quickly. Especially not when he was trying to be the chival-rous one! "Why do you automatically think *they* are taking advantage of *me?*"

"Well…because they're…" *Younger.* "I mean, you're…" *Female.*

He wasn't going to win this one, was he?

"A blind, senile old woman?"

"I never called you senile."

Her smile seemed surprisingly dangerous, for a little, gray-haired matron. "But being old and blind and a woman are still counts against me? I've learned more in all my years than you will ever know, Smith Donnell, and being a woman gives me quite a few advantages, as well, especially when it comes to reading people. I read *you* correctly, didn't I?"

Probably not, according to Arden—who would feel even more guilty about bringing Smith's whole posse into Greta's life than Smith did. What with Smith not doing guilt and all. "I just don't want them—"

"Giving me rides to the market? Do you know how diffi-cult it is to cart groceries on public transit? Or even to read the prices on the shelves? Or do you mean the way they cleared out my gutters, or mowed my back lawn, or fixed that running toilet in my upstairs bathroom? Mitch and Trace have been knights in shining armor, young man. Only one of you has refused me anything."

Smith stared at her for a full two breaths before he realized what she meant. "The *sword?*"

Dreams. Battles. Honor versus love.

"If I can't pass it on to a Kaiser, then at least I can see it go to one of the last honorable members of the Comitatus. You should take it, Smith. You were called to it. It's *meant* for you."

You could give it to Mitch. Or Trace. But for some reason, Smith couldn't bring himself to suggest that. Maybe he *was* selfish, at that.

He told himself it was because he didn't dare out his friends as fellow society members. Oaths of secrecy, and all that. Yeah, that was it.

"Much as I appreciate the offer, Miz Greta, I don't need a sword. Especially not an antique sword. Guns get the job done a lot faster."

"But without as much history. Without as much honor."

Smith shrugged. He was pretty sure they'd covered the him-not-being-that-honorable part already. "No. Thanks anyway. Listen, I'm going to see Arden, try to follow up on her Internet connection to your secret society. Try not to let my friends eat you out of house and home, 'kay?"

"No need to worry about me."

But as Smith headed out, he heard her say, "That's twice."

He turned back, almost stepping on Dido, who tried to follow. "Twice what?"

"Did I say something?" Greta smiled, full of innocence, and called her dog back with a snapped finger. "Ignore me. I'm just an old lady, you know."

Smith narrowed his eyes at her, then realized that—looking straight at him—she couldn't see it, so the gesture was wasted. Now in a thoroughly bad mood, he stalked off toward Arden's recreation center for underprivileged girls. His watch hadn't reached eleven o'clock. yet, and already the August heat suffocated the streets.

Crazy lady.

Stupid antique sword.

He caught himself curling his right hand, as if embracing the memory of the sword's grip, maybe from his dreams. It pissed him off.

A car with air-conditioning, now *that* he could use. Damning proof against the Comitatus would prove equally useful. Good credit. His long-lost trust fund. But an ancient sword, even one with a truly cool alleged lineage? Not so much.

Or so he thought.

Then he turned the corner toward the rec center and found himself with a knife to his throat.

Chapter 7

Smith feinted back, grabbed the wrist that held the knife and twisted. He noticed how slim his attacker's sinewy wrist felt at about the same time that he registered the odd pitch of his gasp.

The knife clattered to the dirty asphalt. Smith stepped on it, looked up and found himself glare to glare with Arden Leigh's baby brother.

The thick, curly black hair—and, to a lesser extent, the expression of disdain—was a dead giveaway.

"Jeff?" God, the kid had grown a foot!

"Stay away from my sister," commanded the teenager through gritted teeth. Smith had to give him points for chutzpah.

"Did you notice that *I* disarmed *you?*" Using his foot, Smith drew the knife across the asphalt, behind him and farther from Jeff. "Speaking of which—what the hell?"

He gave the kid's arm a little shake.

"You dishonored my sister!"

"*What?* If there was any dishonoring going on, I would have noticed." After a moment of further, mutual glaring, Smith got it. "Oh! You mean, when I broke things off."

"And broke into her room last night!"

Oh. Smith remembered that fleeting moment of wariness—a sound? a movement?—that he'd ignored for Arden. He couldn't wholly blame himself. After all…*Arden!*

But it was a wonder he'd survived this long, all the same.

"Your sister handled the matter just fine, kiddo."

"Well, she shouldn't have to. That's what she's got me and Dad for."

Her dad. Smith gritted his teeth at the very thought. He'd disliked Arden's bombastic father long before he quit the Comitatus.

Stay the hell away from my daughter, boyo.

Yeah, right.

Unsure whether he found Arden's brother more chivalrous or chauvinistic—talk about your double-edged swords—Smith shrugged it off. Insults were more fun, anyway. "So how's that knight-errantry working out for you so far?"

"Give me back my knife and I'll show you," Jeff ground out in a fair imitation of *menacing.*

Smith laughed. "Nope."

"It's *my knife!*"

"Yeah, and you used it to threaten *my person.* It's forfeit, buddy." Using one shoulder and arm to block Jeff's sure lunge, Smith dropped into a crouch just long enough to scoop the weapon up, then flipped it in his hand and threw it with deadly accuracy.

The blade embedded itself in a live oak tree, some seventeen feet above the patchy grass and cracked concrete at the tree's base.

Jeff yelled a few ripe words. The kid's frustration undermined Smith's own annoyance. It sucked to lose to someone bigger like this—but every guy had to.

Maybe that was part of the problem with the modern Comitatus. So few of them had the chance to experience *losing*.

Smith interrupted the kid's tirade with, "How long 'til you turn fifteen, Jeff?"

"None of your damned business."

Either way, Smith didn't have a lot of time to try to immunize the kid against some of the Comitatus propaganda—one piece being that Smith was a bad guy. "Want to know where you went wrong?"

"Not attacking you the *last* time you dated my sister?"

"Actually, attacking me at all was pretty stupid. I'm stronger than you, and I've got a hell of a lot more experience. You should never completely trust anyone stronger and more experienced than you." Glancing around, Smith spotted and scooped up a pair of long, dry sticks, also compliments of the live oak. "C'mon," he taunted. "Or are you scared?"

As he'd expected, Jeff Leigh caught the makeshift weapon, too rough to even be called bokken, that he threw.

"Except that I can't trust you." No idiot, Arden's baby brother. *Good.* "Why do you care?"

"Because it would destroy Arden if you ever got yourself killed," admitted Smith, improvising a salute with his stick. Hilt to heart, then to lips, then to the sky, before he spread his arms and gave a small bow, eyes still on the kid. "Knives and swords really can kill, you know. They aren't just symbols. And if you're going to be protecting her, you need to be a *lot* better."

Jeff scowled—but he also lifted his stick, then spread his arms in a half-assed version of Smith's salute. "Like you're so good?"

Ah, the confidence of youth.

Smith hefted his stick, trying not to remember dreams of battle, dreams of a legendary, powerful sword. Then he went on the offense, cutting—well, swinging—toward the kid's right. The kid moved to parry...

And the fight was on.

Arden sensed someone at her office door even before glancing up from her phone call. "I'm so pleased that the evening went well, Ms.—I mean, Molly. The recreational center received some impressive donations, too."

While the state comptroller-slash-gubernatorial candidate related more positive follow-up, Arden watched Val lean into the doorway.

Arden mouthed, *Is it important?*

Val whispered, "Oh, honey." The mixture of amusement and disbelief in those words drove all images of a new female governor for Texas out of Arden's thoughts. She escaped with a few more polite murmurings and swept out of her office after her friend and partner.

Val hadn't been smiling, but that wasn't surprising.

The twist of the darker woman's lips was enough. "You've got to see this to believe it," she promised.

So Arden followed her through an expanding cluster of interested teenage girls, past the fenced edge of the rec center's property...

...to the sight of Smith Donnell playing pirate with Arden's little brother, Jeff.

Swashbuckling pirate.

They took sideways steps toward and then away from each other with each clash of...branches.

"Attack sword-first," Smith chided. "Defend body-first."

Jeff said a word that he shouldn't, and Arden frowned. The teenage girls behind her giggled their approval.

Smith said, "Your mouth wasn't on that list. Try again," and thwapped Jeff on the upper arm with his stick.

If those had been real swords, Jeff would be bleeding—but

they weren't. Her brother was fairly safe. Just *how* safe he seemed surprised Arden. Apparently she trusted Smith more than she would have thought.

She didn't giggle like a teenager. But, watching Smith's athletic expertise, she found herself pressing her lips together to stop a smile. His footwork alone…

"He can *fence?*" murmured Val.

Arden nodded. "He and his friends were on the fencing team in college."

"Gotta love a man who's good with his sword."

Arden shushed her friend a little too sharply, but flushed—she'd never experienced Smith's "sword" herself. That was no cause for embarrassment, was it?

After they'd broken up, the lack of that particular memory had been a relief. Bad enough that the melodrama of their imbalanced courtship had begun to dominate her life, her dreams. By the time their last six-month trial period had drawn toward an end, she'd longed for their consummation as much as she'd hoped for a ring.

When he dumped her, she'd been glad not to have given up that last, significant piece of ground. Bad enough to lose her heart without feeling cheapened, as well.

Today, watching the play of his shoulder muscles under his worn T-shirt, his blue-jeaned thighs as he danced in and out of Jeff's reach, she couldn't help but remember how those shoulders had felt under her greedy hands last night, how those legs had felt pressed against hers. And the sight of his patience with Jeff!

"A horizontal block for a vertical strike," Smith reminded her brother. As Jeff raised his branch over his head, Smith poked him gently in the ribs. "And a vertical block for a horizontal strike. Come on, that's as basic as it gets."

Jeff swung his stick downward a little too violently. Luckily, Smith, practicing what he preached, stopped the arcing blow with a horizontal block. The wood made a loud crack at impact, and bits of dust and bark flew off.

"Enough!" Arden declared in her authority voice, stepping out from the crowd. "We have a no-violence rule at Girls First."

Jeff obediently lowered his stick.

Smith smacked him lightly across the butt. "Hah! Don't get distracted."

"With her dressed like that?" protested Jeff. Arden looked down at herself in confusion—standard jeans, a ruched cotton top—and heard another smack.

"Hah-ha," Jeff sing-songed back at Smith, who, when Arden looked back up, was rubbing his arm and looking sheepish. And great. The exercise had flushed him with vitality…and the memory of his lips on her, last night, didn't exactly distract her from his already handsome form.

"Very funny," Smith chided Jeff—and a belated piece of memory clicked into place.

"Girls," instructed Arden, "please go on back into the air-conditioning. There's no more to see here."

"I want to learn how to do that," protested Latashya Jones, lingering.

"We'll see what we can do to add fencing to our activities. But for now—Val?"

Val stepped in, herding their charges out of earshot, and Arden turned on her menfolk.

Especially the shorter one.

"Is this tomorrow, Jeff?"

Smith looked confused. She didn't care.

"I specifically told you not to come down here today."

"Because he was coming today, right?" Any camaraderie she'd sensed between Jeff and Smith vanished.

"That is none of your business, young man. I have the right to see whomever I wish, whenever I wish."

"Exactly," said Smith. "That's why I was fighting him. As your, you know…champion."

Knowing a lie when she heard it—especially when his eyes danced like that—she was careful to use her most scathing tone to say, "My hero." Even if something about the idea of Smith as her champion gave her a fleeting, not-unpleasant warmth.

In lieu of turning on herself for such idiocy, she turned on him. "And, you! If you ever lift a hand against my baby brother again—"

"Arden!" protested Jeff, flushing.

Some of the girls still clustered around her giggled.

"I *am* calling the police. And no, it doesn't matter that you were just using sticks. Even sticks can be dangerous. Weapons are *never* the answer."

For some reason, Smith looked intently at Jeff as he said, "You're right, Arden. I apologize."

Jeff just glared. "Why's *he* allowed to be here?"

"Still none of your business, but it's because I invited him."

"You said you two broke up."

"We did. We have business today, not pleasure."

Jeff's narrowed eyes didn't seem to believe her, but she wasn't the one who had planned an ambush at work. She didn't owe him explanations about whom she saw—even in her room—or why.

He was the child here!

Smith, curse him, said, "Not that any time with your sister, even for business, could fail to be pleasurable."

Arden scowled at him.

He grinned back, unfazed. Tousled. *Sexy.*

Sugar.

Smith supposed it made sense that any meeting with a conspiracy theorist would be shrouded in mystery. But the

plan that Arden explained to him two days later put everything
in favor of her elusive Internet source, Vox07, instead of them.

Or it would, if Smith didn't have a couple of secret weapons.

"He said to come alone," worried Arden, shifting uncomfortably in her seat at the West End barbecue restaurant that
overlooked the downtown Dallas light-rail line. Despite the
historic district's popularity, with its brick streets and restored-
warehouse shops, they were the only customers using the
patio seating—with the exception of a skinny teenaged girl
reading a paperback. But Smith didn't think the summer tem-
peratures were the cause of Arden's discomfort, and not just
because the restaurant's outdoor fans helped push the August
heat around some.

"They *always* say to come alone." He hadn't lied to Jeff.
Considering how little he would get of it, time spent with
Arden was a real pleasure. He loved watching how neatly she
managed to eat something as messy as a pulled-chicken sand-
wich. He loved how, when he asked for the salt, she passed
both it and the pepper with one hand, as if the pair should
never be separated—she'd always done that. She'd always
done a lot of little, delightful, *proper* things.

Which had always made her improprieties all the tastier.

Even after a year, he remembered how she liked her iced
tea—sweet—which she now sipped delicately. "Won't Vox re-
fuse to talk to me, once he knows that I lied?"

"He might." Seeing that he'd already plowed through his
barbecued brisket, while Arden had taken only a few nibbles
of her own late lunch, Smith forced himself to slow down on
the fries. Just because he was hungry didn't mean she had to
know it. "But he wants to know what *you* know, too."

"Wouldn't him refusing to talk invalidate our entire reason
for coming here?" Arden, on the other hand, seemed far less
enamored of her time with Smith. That made sense. He hadn't
just burned their bridges when his exile from the Comitatus

had prompted him to set her free. Drunk. Over the phone. From a bar.

He'd kind of blown those bridges to smithereens.

Then he'd burned the smithereens.

Of course he was still in love with her. These last few days in her company only emphasized how depressingly little that had changed. But apparently he'd done his job in alienating her too well. Sure, she'd kissed him the other night. A momentary weakness. A goodbye.

She'd *stopped* kissing him, too.

So. Business. Vox07, the mysterious Internet stranger who may have narced Arden's investigation out to the Comitatus in the first place. Arden had let Smith read the e-mails Vox07 had sent her asking for a meeting to trade further information. The stranger knew a lot about the Comitatus to not *be* Comitatus.

Especially since Mitch's attempt to trace the informant's e-mail had led to a sophisticated series of feints, blinds and remote servers.

"What would invalidate our reason for being here," Smith said, once he'd finished chewing and swallowing, "would be letting someone hurt you in an attempt to shut you up. And if you came alone, that might just happen."

"Well, thank heavens I have a big, strong man to protect me," she drawled, only the simmer in her eyes giving away her sarcasm.

"More than one," Smith assured her.

Arden twisted in her seat again, scanning the small crowd waiting under the arched shade canopies that marked a stop along the overhead electric lines and near-invisible, street-level tracks. "What? Where?"

"Don't *look* for them." Smith took some pride in the fact that even he had to work to notice Trace and Mitch, despite Trace's size and Mitch's gold hair. "This Vox guy might let you get by with one guard, but not three."

"Which is why I wouldn't have brought them in the first place!"

"Considering that someone held a knife to your throat not three days ago, you'd be stupid not to."

Arden lifted her iced-tea glass to her lips but paused before taking a sip, her gaze dry. The expression made a delightful contrast against her sleeveless pink sundress. "However did I survive an entire year without your charming advice?"

"Hah! So you *do* know it wasn't three years." But before he could pursue that delightful discovery further—or, worse, flirt more obviously—Smith turned toward the faint wail of an approaching light-rail train. "It's showtime, folks."

The plan, as outlined by Vox07, was for Arden to wait here at the restaurant, in the open, for the 2:18 p.m. southbound, red-line train. Once Vox saw that she was alone—more or less—he would join her on the patio, where they could trade what information they'd gathered about the Comitatus.

"I'll be just inside this doorway, listening," Smith assured her, clearing his dishes as he stood. Since his impoverishment, he'd taken more than one job doing just that. "If you're at all uncomfortable, twirl your hair around your finger, got it?"

Arden smiled pure honey up at him through the afternoon sunshine—and Smith just about dropped the dishes he was holding. Damn, she really was the most beautiful woman in the world. And he had to be the most stupid man, to have let her go. He barely heard her tease, "Are you certain you don't want me to tap out a message in Morse code with my dinner knife?"

"No." His own voice sounded faint in his ears. "The prearranged signal's fine."

Arden blinked, seeming confused—but by then the train was in sight, so Smith ducked into the restaurant and took over a booth by the window, so that he could watch the confrontation. The sleek white and yellow train slid into the station, sounding its horn to counter the near silence of its electric cars and warn unwary pedestrians away from the tracks.

A handful of passengers disembarked. Several, carrying backpacks or books, immediately headed toward El Centro Community College. Three, still wearing name tags from some conference or another, headed toward the West End's pedestrian-only brick streets. Two were tourists, from their digital cameras to their matching *Everything is Bigger in Texas* T-shirts. One swarthy young man looked fairly suspicious as he headed their way, until Smith recognized the apron sticking out of his pocket and realized that he probably bussed tables. And…

And that was it. With more bells and a strained whistle, the train slid back into silent motion in the direction of the Grassy Knoll, Union Station and parts south.

Arden sat alone at her outdoor table, as if jilted.

Again.

She wore it well, arching an eyebrow at her iced tea without commenting, but still…

Hell.

Some instinct in Smith had him wait—you never could tell if this Vox guy wasn't careful enough to come on the next train, or by bus, or from one of the other restaurants or shops. Which meant Smith had been an idiot to spend any time near Arden at all…but damn. Could he have given up even a minute more of it?

Time stretched. In the far distance, a northbound train sounded its whistle to warn of its approach.

Arden succeeded in not glancing toward the window where Smith waited, watching. She did glance at the reading teenager, probably wondering about her opinion on all-girl youth centers, until her subject scowled, turned down the page on her book, shouldered her backpack and got up to go.

The girl stumbled beside Arden—

And dropped something in her purse.

Smith almost didn't see her clever sleight of hand. As it was, he barely moved fast enough to block the doorway back into the restaurant.

The teenager, deerlike in her thinness and the skittish way she leaped back, had long, chocolate-colored hair that all but hid her expression. Still, Smith could read body language.

He could read her fear.

"Hiya, Vox," he said, saving the cursing of himself for his assumptions about Vox07's gender and age for later.

Still seated at her table, Arden parted her perfect lips in surprise.

Vox ran.

Just like that, before Smith could toss out a single quip, the teenager darted across the patio and vaulted the iron fencing that encircled it, despite the short, flowy skirt she wore—or the cowboy boots. She raced toward the light-rail stop. Smith took off after her, swinging over the fence with somewhat less agility than Little Deer-Girl, but damn, she was fast.

She probably would have shot across the tracks and lost herself in the El Centro crowd if it hadn't been for the Comitatus. One minute, the girl was in full flight. The next, she'd stumbled to a stop—face-to-face with Prescott Lowell, who'd appeared from behind the handicap-access ramp beside the tracks.

Now Smith *really* cursed himself. Obviously, despite whatever knowledge she claimed to have about the Comitatus, Vox07 wasn't part of a secret society of all-powerful males. Somehow, he and Arden must have led the Comitatus here.

Lowell wore a suit—Hugo Boss. In August. Even without brandishing a knife, he might as well have worn a pin reading *Hi, I'm Prescott. Ask Me About My Secret Society.*

Vox07 took one look at him and whirled around to backtrack. Then she saw Smith—and froze.

"It's all right, honey!" Arden's voice surprised Smith, not the least because she swept past him in a pink blur, heading toward the girl. She must have run, too. How could Arden look so good after running in this heat? "You can trust us. Come—"

But a whistle, overloud and startling in its nearness, drowned out her voice.

Seeing what was about to happen, Smith lunged forward.

The girl, as if in shock, took one step backward—more firmly onto the light-rail tracks that bisected the brick street, just as the northbound train bore down on her.

Arden surged forward, blind to the risk to herself—and Smith, seeing everything unfold too fast to stop it, too fast to get there, did the only thing he could. He ran. He couldn't reach the teenager. God help him, he couldn't. But he might reach Arden before she ended up on the tracks, as well.

Brakes shrieked. Someone yelled. The train's whistle howled into one long, panicked scream.

Smith reached—and caught Arden. He dragged her forcefully into his arms, spinning to put himself between her and the blur of white and yellow that barreled by them where the teenaged girl had been standing.

The girl they'd chased onto the tracks.

He muffled Arden's cry against his chest, muffled his own silent scream somewhere far deeper, far more dangerous.

The breeze off the train blew his hair. He could feel its heat, far worse than that of August, push against his back. With his head ducked, he could see a white stripe under his old shoes and Arden's strappy sandals, her neatly painted toes.

The safety line of demarcation separating the public from the train.

Smith closed his eyes for a moment, inhaling the magnolia scent of Arden's thick black hair, selfishly glad for her safety even as the train's horn fell silent and the crowd's shouts took over.

He held on to her. She clutched him. And God help him, he was glad that she'd survived, no matter what had happened to the teenaged informant he and the Comitatus may have just helped kill. Maybe his so-called *noble* bloodline was corrupt down to the cells, at that.

So much for being a hero.

Chapter 8

Arden, tucked forcibly into Smith's chest, could barely breathe. She'd never felt so terrible. Not when she'd seen such horrific poverty, on a good-will tour as a pageant finalist, that she'd had to save little girls and thus discovered her mission in life. Not when Smith, whom she'd thought she loved, dumped her with no explanation. Not even when her stepmother died.

None of those had been her fault.

But this…!

Someone began to shout at them—a Dallas Area Rapid Transit cop. Arden couldn't make out the angry words through her shock, though clearly the stocky woman was scolding them for what had happened. As if they'd meant for it to happen? As if they didn't know…?

Maybe Smith did understand. He drew her gently back from beside, *right* beside, the northbound train. For the first time, Arden saw how he'd stepped between her and danger, how close he'd come to being hit himself.

Nausea tightened her throat. She held on to his hard arms for balance now—and more.

Then, strangely, with another shriek of its whistle—the train pulled forward.

To reach the poor girl? Surely not just to…leave? Unwilling to see, but less willing to avoid what they'd done, Arden twisted far enough from Smith's arms to see the tracks as the light-rail train picked up speed and slid away in a yellow and white sequence.

She saw nothing but brick and rails.

"Smith," she gasped, noting a definite paleness to his usually tanned face. He hadn't wanted to see the carnage, either. Somehow, that realization softened something inside her, something hard that over the weekend had seemed to melt a little more, the more time she spent time with him. "Where is she?"

The DART cop continued to shout at them—and at someone else.

Belatedly, Smith loosened his grip on Arden and moved his gaze past the empty bricks to the sight of a big, swarthy man their age. She recognized Smith's friend, Trace Beaudry, climbing up from the bricks and dragging the teenager by one slim hand.

"—*doing*?" Trace demanded, bent over the stunned girl as if to deliberately intimidate her. "When a train's about to hit you, you *move,* you don't just *stand* there!"

"Oh, thank God!" Arden pulled from Smith's dumbfounded stillness to hurry across the tracks and gather the girl away from her oversized rescuer. But the girl flinched away from Arden's touch, back against Trace. "We didn't mean to frighten you," Arden insisted.

"Sorry, Arden," quipped another familiar voice—Smith's old friend Mitch Talbott. All they needed now was the nebbish Quinn to round out the quartet. But Quinn didn't seem to be nearby. That, or the light-haired Mitch just grabbed more attention. "I guess you don't have the way with women that Trace does."

Trace seemed to like the teasing even less than Arden. "Yeah, well, my way kept her from being run over by Smith's damned legacy."

Smith's…?

"My family was in railroads, not rapid transit," Smith defended himself. Ah. The *Donnell* legacy. Arden watched him draw every bit of it around himself, despite his old T-shirt and jeans, as he spun on the transit cop. "Yes, we get it, no playing chase across the train tracks, won't happen again, are you happy?"

Since the woman drew her ticket book from her back pocket, Arden presumed she was not. Speaking of certain individuals' way with women… "Let me handle this," she suggested to the men. "Just get her…Vox…" What was the girl's name? "Take her somewhere that she can catch her breath, all right?"

"No!" So the girl could speak after all. She glanced frantically around them before turning her imploring gaze back to Trace. "Not with them, not…."

Then the girl's eyes widened, rolled upward, and she sank toward the ground.

Trace caught her before she made it all the way. After a moment of apparent confusion, he lifted her with disturbing ease. "Crap."

But at least it distracted the DART officer from ticketing them.

They got Vox07 back to the barbecue restaurant—in the air-conditioned shade, not the patio. Trace reluctantly held her in his lap until Arden's attentions, dabbing the girl's temples with a napkin dipped in ice water and fanning her with a menu, revived her. The girl's eyes fluttered, and she stiffened. Then, when Trace unceremoniously slid her onto the bench seat between him and Arden, she caught sight of him and seemed to relax—marginally—even as she stared.

Arden couldn't imagine anyone ever having that reaction to a man she'd always thought of as thuggish, but if Trace kept Vox07—or whatever her name was—calm, more power to him.

"Here's some sweet tea," she murmured, moving the straw to the girl's lips until Vox took both cup and straw from her and obediently drank. Their waitress had been wonderfully solicitous when they'd lied and blamed the heat—not an uncommon cause of fainting spells around here. "Don't try to talk right away. Nobody's going to hurt you."

The girl drank—but her narrow-eyed gaze, from behind her veil of long hair, radiated distrust of all of them, Arden included.

That unnerved Arden. Not almost-killed-by-a-train unnerved, but still. She was a Leigh, of the Highland Park Leighs. She had a way with people. She was charming—except sometimes with Smith, who brought out the worst in her, but that was hardly her fault. Excluding him, being good with people was her *thing*.

Now Smith, who sat directly across the plank table from Arden, made a huffing noise. He slumped back on the bench seat he shared with Mitch, and his feet tangled with hers. Deliberately? "So if she's not going to talk, what are we supposed to do?"

"Eat?" Trace rudely helped himself to one of the complimentary corn chips the waitress had brought for them.

"Anyone bring a deck of cards?" suggested Mitch in that joking way of his. "Nothing tops off a near-death experience like a good game of Go Fish."

"Patience is a sign of maturity," Arden reminded them sweetly, through gritted teeth. "Trace, perhaps you should leave some chips for her. Salt helps counteract the heat."

"She didn't faint from the heat," Smith reminded her right back. "She fainted from fear. C'mon, Ard. You saw Prescott

Lowell, didn't you? How do you suppose he got here, unless he followed you?"

Did he always get this annoying after close calls? "Hmm. Let me use my psychic skills." Arden dropped the dampened napkin to turn on him. "*I don't know.* We already established that he's Comitatus."

The girl made a snorting sound, like, *duh.*

Smith leaned across the table in his apparent need to push his point home. "The longer you and Vox here are out in the open like this, the more vulnerable you are."

"Vox is a stupid name," noted Trace, between chips.

Finally the girl spoke. Her voice was faint—but she spoke. With sarcasm. "Not my real name."

"So tell us your real name," insisted Smith, with his usual lack of tact.

The girl shook her head, her eyes only touching on him before wandering across the table to touch on—and veer from—Mitch. Then Trace. "Lowell is Comitatus. Not the only one. You led him here. Lied to me."

She said that last with her gaze planted firmly on Arden.

Arden felt her heart sink at the truth of the accusation. "I'm sorry, honey. I know you said to come alone—"

"Don't apologize!" Smith interrupted, as if she needed defending against even a teenager. "You'd rather you both were here alone with Lowell?"

"Perhaps we could have handled him," noted Arden.

"Maybe you couldn't have," insisted Smith.

"Maybe you two—" this last came from Mitch "—could take this to your own table? This was supposed to be the quiet, calming-down-after-the-excitement table. Not to mention, you're attracting attention. Jenny's been so nice. Don't make her tell us all to leave."

Jenny was their waitress.

Flushing at the idea of having lost her poise so seriously,

much less in public, Arden drew in a breath to protest that she could control herself—but Smith had already stood and circled to the table immediately behind her. All she had to do was turn on her bench seat, sweeping her gored skirt with her, and she was facing him.

"What's your problem?" he demanded, voice lowered.

"I don't have a problem." *Except you.* For some reason, she wasn't as anxious to add the usual dig.

He widened his brown eyes, impatient. "Then why are you acting like this?"

"Because you could have been killed!" The accusation slipped from her lips before Arden even recognized the truth of it. But, hearing it, she accepted it. *That* was her problem, all right. She could only take comfort in the fact that her voice didn't shake. It came out a little strident, perhaps. But no shaking. "You put yourself between me and the train," she clarified, even more calmly. "You could have been killed."

Trace, behind them, snorted. "No kidding."

Smith glared at his friend's broad back before returning his gaze to Arden. His eyes softened, just to touch on her. "Well, I wasn't."

"But you could have been."

"And Vox over there could have been run over," Smith reminded her.

"Or me," Trace reminded both of them over his shoulder. "I could've been run over."

"Or Trace," Smith conceded with a shrug. "But nobody was."

"This time!" That definitely sounded strident.

Smith squinted across the table at her. "Are you mad at me again? Because this time, I had nothing to do with… Well, barely anything… Just stop being mad, already!"

"I'm not." *Dogs get mad, people get angry.* "I'm… worried."

"I won't let anything happen to you, so— Ouch!" That last

came when she reached across the table and smacked him in the upper arm with a menu. "That felt mad."

"I'm worried about *you,* you idiot!" Saying it forced her to face reality. Whether she should care about this handsome, foolish, gallant, *stupid* idiot was immaterial. Even if he didn't deserve her sympathy, she did care.

She cared a great deal. Again. Still.

Sugar.

"I don't want to see you hurt," she continued, less certain of herself.

"I don't want to see you hurt, either," Smith insisted. "So we're even. So what's the problem?"

I'd only just begun to get over you, and now…

But she most certainly would not discuss that in front of his friends, her young conspiracy contact *or* Jenny the waitress. "Can we just call it nerves?" she suggested.

For once, Smith had nothing snarky to say. Instead, he just studied her, then shrugged, as if shaking off her insanity.

To end the uncomfortable conversation, Arden simply turned back to the original table, leaving him to circle to his original seat. Mitch grinned at all of them, far too cheerfully.

Vox07 said, "None of you sound Comitatus. Too disorganized. Too emotional."

Arden stared at her. *What?*

And the entire energy at the table changed.

"*We* don't sound Comitatus?" asked Smith, even as he thought, *How did she guess?* And then doubling back to the previous few minutes of encouragement, *Arden didn't want to see me hurt.* But mostly, sticking with the present, *How did she guess?*

When she'd said Lowell wasn't the only one, Vox07 had *known.*

Still, Smith winced a little when Trace snorted his innocence and protested, "Who's Comitatus?" Great. Invite the conspiracy expert to start naming names.

"You think these three are part of an all-powerful secret society?" Arden's dimpled smile reassured Smith, but she didn't have to sound quite *that* amused. "*Them?* No wonder you were frightened, poor thing."

She reached for the teenager's hand, but the girl pulled away, fixing her eyes, still half-hidden behind straight, unstyled hair, on Smith. "Who are you?"

They hadn't done introductions yet, what with her having been unconscious. "Smith Donnell."

"*Donnell.*" She nodded, but didn't look at all satisfied as she turned toward Mitch, collected his surname of Talbott, and continued on to Trace. For the first time since he'd yanked her from death on the tracks, she looked frightened of him.

"Trace Beaudry," he said firmly, as if speaking to an idiot. "And I'm not Comitatus."

I'm not. Now Smith understood the hair Trace was splitting. Trace had come late into the privileged lifestyle. After his birth father disowned him for betraying the Comitatus, Trace had disowned his father right back—and gone back to his original name. Apparently, he thought you could divorce vows, too.

"Beaudry," the girl repeated—but without the dour weight she'd given Arden, Smith and Mitch's last names. This was amazing. She must have an entire roll sheet of Comitatus memorized. Even Smith couldn't have recognized fellow members just by their names. "Beaudry?"

Trace's look dared her to contradict him. "Beaudry."

"Why are you with them?" *Them* included Arden. Arden obviously didn't understand why. And Smith wanted to get a handle on this day of revelations before their little conspiracy theorist outed everyone—up to and including Arden's father—to a woman not yet ready to know the truth. It was one thing for Leigh to be a self-righteous jerk. It was another to force Arden to see it if she didn't have to.

"It's a long story, conspiracy girl, and not one we need to be discussing in a public restaurant with Prescott Lowell and who knows who else lurking outside. We've got to get to some kind of safe zone before we go any further."

"Greta's house," suggested Trace, then shrugged when the others looked at him. "Hey, she said she'd be frying chicken."

"Greta's house," repeated the teenager softly, as if to herself. "The woman Arden Leigh asked about. Kaiser. Comitatus name. Might as well be Stuart."

"We could go somewhere else," Arden reassured her. "Perhaps—"

"Until sixty years ago." The girl nodded. "Greta's house."

Oookay. Smith could see that she would be oodles of fun. "Well, then. Mitch and Trace drove in, but it's probably not a good idea for Vox—look, whiz kid, we can't keep calling you Vox or Vox07. We gave you our names. What the hell is yours?"

Arden's mouth fell open in rebuke. "Smith Donnell!"

"What, we've got two Smith Donnells?" quipped Mitch, and was soundly ignored.

The girl looked at Trace, who rolled his eyes and growled, "We could just call you Shorty."

"Sibyl," she admitted. "Won't tell my last name. Sibyl's distinctive enough."

And Smith had thought *he'd* gotten paranoid since his exile from the Comitatus? "You might want to stick with Shorty. Anyway, I'm not sending a teenager who isn't ours in a car with two strange men. Shut up," he added, before Mitch could jump on *strange*. "No matter how honorable they are. No offense."

Vox—that is, Sibyl—said, "I'm not a teenager."

"Since I'm guessing you aren't going anywhere without Trace, weird though *that* is, Arden can ride with Mitch. Trace and I will take the train to the Westmoreland stop with our little informant here. Any questions? No? Good."

He said that last part impractically fast, standing to make it so, dropping too much cash—goodbye, sweet money—on the table so they wouldn't have to wait for their lunch check.

Of course, it couldn't be *that* easy—certainly not considering how Arden arched that beautiful back of hers. "What if Sibyl doesn't want to take the train, considering it almost killed her?"

"Safe *inside*," Sibyl reminded her darkly, leaving out the implied *you idiot*. "Comitatus almost killed me."

"Good," repeated Smith. "Then—"

"And wouldn't it be smarter for me to accompany Sibyl and Trace?" Arden's smile, still aimed at Smith, looked more feral by the moment. "Wouldn't she feel safer with a woman?"

Smith's problem was that Arden's suggestion *did* make the most sense. The only reason he was trying to send her off with Mitch was to buy some time. He had to convince the kid not to tell Arden that her father was Comitatus.

Or that Smith and Mitch were, either. On the tiny chance Arden couldn't see the flashing signs. That would be nice.

He couldn't exactly use that argument right here.

Luckily, Sibyl handled the smaller problem on her own, her dark gaze briefly but deliberately touching on Arden. "Wouldn't feel safer with you."

The only sign that the girl's blunt statement hurt was how completely Arden's expression stilled.

That, and the way Mitch said, "Ouch."

Smith felt the insult like a gut punch, and decided he didn't like their little informant. At all. Only sheer pragmatism kept him from pointing out just how amazingly wrong the girl was in her character assessment. Instead of jumping to Arden's defense, he made a show of helping her up, like the lady she was, and used the moment of nearness—and her warmth, and her magnolia scent—to whisper private encouragement.

"Is it my imagination, or is she not all there?"

As he'd hoped, the stillness of Arden's hidden pain eased into a more natural expression for her—disapproval of him. "Don't be rude," she murmured back, too good a person to return even Sibyl's dislike with her own. "We don't know what the poor thing has endured at the hands of these Comitatus people."

But he thought, hoped, he detected some relief, as well. "If you say so."

"Good manners don't cost anything."

And he couldn't help himself. He ducked in front of her and kissed the prim right off her full, luscious lips.

Arden neither protested nor pulled away. She didn't exactly throw him onto one of the plank tables and have her wild way with him, either. But he'd take what encouragement he could. And he was definitely encouraged by how her lips softened against his.

Stupid timing.

"See you two back at Greta's, then," he said cheerfully, drawing back from Arden's blank surprise—and her still-parted lips. "Be careful."

"She'll be safe with me." Mitch gently took Arden's elbow and guided her easily toward the main exit. "The car's this way. You may like her. I rebuilt most of her from parts I got at the scrap yards off Jefferson…."

Yes. Arden so enjoyed patchwork automobiles. Still, Smith wasn't going to waste the moment, and turned immediately to Sibyl. "Look—"

"You're Comitatus," she announced flat out, now that Arden was at a safe distance. "Son of William Donnell. Grandson of Wesley Donnell. Descended from the railroad king Donnells." She considered that. "You don't want her to know."

"That's right. I don't—not the Comitatus part. So what's it going to take for you to keep your mouth shut about who in our immediate circle, including her father, may or may not be secret society?"

All the girl said was, "Secrets are for cowards."

Great.

Prescott Lowell, in the shade of a sunglasses kiosk, snapped a few camera-phone pictures as the conclave divided into two parties. He didn't recognize the skinny bit of white trash who had almost gotten herself flattened by the blue-line, and he didn't really care. She was a girl. Like Arden Leigh, she would matter only if she became trouble.

And Arden Leigh, just as he had expected, had become a great deal of trouble.

Lowell didn't recognize the men she was with, either. Not personally. But by description? Especially here in the Dallas/Fort Worth metroplex?

The first two—the pale-haired surfer type and the swarthy giant—could have been anyone. But the quick-moving fellow who appeared to be in charge and, more significantly, appeared to be remarkably attached to Arden Leigh?

The same Arden Leigh who'd dated Will Donnell's son, Smith, until the troublemaker had gotten himself exiled?

So Lowell's elders thought curious daughters were no great threat. They had ways of diverting her, did they? As he'd believed all along, he was right and they, in their old-fashioned sentiments, were wrong.

This curious daughter was fraternizing with at least one Comitatus exile—behind everyone's back but his own.

All Lowell had to do was decide exactly when to put this information to its best use, to facilitate his own rise within the inner circles, to where the real power waited.

And to destroy anyone who had impeded him.

Now *that*—that would be power.

Chapter 9

Arden was no idiot. She'd caught the significance behind Sibyl's murmured comments. *Preston Lowell wasn't the only Comitatus member. None of Smith's friends sounded like Comitatus.* Her first reaction had been shocked amusement. But the more she thought about the girl's claims...

Arden found the denial more difficult to maintain than she had expected.

She would be able to piece more together if Mitch would just *stop talking* for a minute.

Not likely, that.

"So you and Smith, huh?" He had to call the cheerful question over the rush of the open windows. "I mean—*you*. And Smith. That's good to see. He's been damned hard to live with, harder to live with anyway, since the two of you split."

Right. As if Smith hadn't done the splitting himself. Not that they were together now. "Mitch—"

"I like seeing something good come out of this last year,"

he continued loudly, his hands easy but skilled on the steering wheel. The brown wheel did not match the rest of the car's blue interior. Arden began to suspect that he really had rebuilt this old sedan from a scrap yard. But it ran.

And it had seat belts, albeit no air-conditioning. Seventy miles per hour kept them marginally comfortable.

"About that," she tried, raising her voice, but he interrupted her again.

"I've got to say, this puts you in an even better light, too, considering. Not that you aren't one of those people who seems to have her very own heavenly lighting crew at all times, but still. A lot of women won't have anything to do with a guy unless he's got the money to back it up."

So—Smith *was* poor. As, to judge by his ride, was Mitch. She'd suspected as much, considering how poorly they dressed of late, but it had been hard to imagine and impolite to ask.

"Why did Sibyl imply that you were Comitatus?"

"What's that?"

She felt certain he'd heard her, but fingered a tendril of blowing hair out of her mouth and repeated the question more loudly.

Mitch glanced quickly from the road to her, then back, showing dimples. "Did she imply that? Maybe you misheard—"

"Yes, she implied that." Arden disliked having to interrupt, but it seemed the only way she would get answers. Trace had already denied the accusation, and, in any case, Arden saw him as least likely among them to have the subtlety or clout to be allowed into a powerful secret society. But the other two? This was too important. She cranked her window up, glaring at Mitch until he did the same. The temperature in the car immediately spiked, but the relative silence was worth it. "Is it you, or is it…?" She swallowed. She could say it. "Is it Smith?"

Mitch glanced into the rearview mirror and said, "Oh, look. Prescott Lowell is tailing us." He almost sounded relieved.

Arden turned in her seat, looked out the back window. A pickup truck followed them, not unusual in Dallas. But behind that, in another lane, came a dark sedan.

She supposed it could be Prescott Lowell. Or it could be a stalling tactic.

In any case, she refused to be distracted further. Settling back into her passenger seat, surprisingly comfortable and clean, Arden repeated, "Are you or Smith Comitatus, Mitch?"

Mitch slanted his blue eyes toward her, then back to the road. Then to her again. She allowed the silence to loom, louder and louder.

He had to blink first. "I can honestly tell you that at this time neither of us is a member of any secret society," he admitted finally.

Arden began to relax, to smile at her own paranoia—until she recognized what he didn't say. *At this time?* So at some other time, the answer might have been different.

The possibility made her go very, very still inside. It shouldn't have. She should have recognized it a lot earlier— what had Smith said? *I had a disagreement with some of my associates. They had more clout, and I lost.*

He'd lost everything.

"I mean, you said so yourself," Mitch continued nervously. "How ridiculous is that? Sure, we were rich, but we aren't special. Right? What business would we have, being drafted into a hereditary organization, rubbing elbows with important people, doing anything like that?" But neither of those sounded especially unlikely, certainly not a year ago. *"Taking vows of lifelong secrecy?"* His chuckle sounded strained. "It is to laugh."

Vows of *lifelong secrecy.* Meaning…

Was he agreeing with her? Without breaking any vows?

Arden stopped asking questions. She wasn't sure she had the voice to ask more, anyway. Smith was—had been—part of a secret society.

Unless Mitch was teasing. Mitch teased quite a bit.

He looked remarkably serious, in the driver's seat. For him.

The possibilities and their assorted consequences dizzied Arden in a way that had nothing to do with Mitch's driving, or the mirror flashes of August sunlight off highway windshields or the increasingly close heat in the un-air-conditioned car. Smith, her Smith, had been Comitatus. And, to judge by his current circumstances, he had left the same way Greta Kaiser's father had left.

Exiled.

Could it possibly be for as good a reason?

A matter of honor, he'd said.

Arden knew she could suffer from selective blindness when it came to people she loved—but this was Smith! She didn't… That is, she hadn't meant to…

What if he really was a hero, after all?

"So." Mitch glanced into the rearview again. "Do you like going fast?"

"Excuse me?" When she realized what he meant, though, Arden laughed at her own prim tone. "I'm told you're a good driver."

"Lies. I'm a great driver." Mitch grinned, cranking down his window and raising his voice. "Let's lose this guy. Stupid, secret-society scum."

With very little coaxing, his car leaped forward at the same time that he changed lanes.

And lose him they did.

Even Trace was unable to get a promise from the decidedly odd little Sibyl that she would not expose anyone else's involvement in the secret society. On their train ride into Oak

Cliff, Smith tried coaxing. He pointed out how hurt Arden would be to learn the truth about her father. Chivalry or not, he might have tried threatening the kid, if she weren't already wound as tight as a lemur on caffeine. It wasn't that she fidgeted or moved quickly. On the walk from the station to Greta Kaiser's house, she gave every indication of being still and observant. But Smith could feel the tension roiling off of her all the same.

"You can find your way back, if you need to?" he asked as they turned a corner, him and Trace flanking her. "Not that we won't take you home, but you do know where you are, right?"

She gave him a *gee, you're stupid* look from behind her hair before she went back to surveying the mix of old homes, both renovated and crumbling, around them. "Oak Cliff. Location of the historic Texas Theater." She looked down to watch her feet, in scuffed cowboy boots that didn't go with her short, flowy skirt, as she walked. "Where Lee Harvey Oswald was captured after assassinating President John F. Kennedy." She looked back up, quite serious. *"Or so they say."*

Here was an encouraging thought. Maybe Arden wouldn't believe the kid, even if she *did* tell all.

Arden and Mitch weren't there yet, which concerned Smith. Greta, on the other hand, was thrilled to have yet another guest for dinner as, of course, was her dog, with whom Sibyl immediately bonded— "Dido. The *Aeneid?*"

Great. The air in Greta's house already felt weird, charged. Smith couldn't turn around without some part of him tracking that damned hidden sword, like a compass always knowing which way was north. He didn't like his suspicion that his continued dreams of battle, of love—of betrayal—had connection. Aeneas had dumped his lover. She'd killed herself over it.

Not exactly a role model, despite the whole founding-a-new-empire business.

Luckily Mitch's gray hobby-mobile pulled up in front of the house before Smith's concern reached call-her-cell-phone proportions. Mitch and Arden took turns praising how skillfully Mitch had eluded Prescott Lowell's attempt to tail them, so cheerfully that at first Smith didn't even notice anything different in Arden.

He was too busy recognizing the suspicion that he felt as jealousy. That had to be why he inserted himself between Arden and Mitch as they settled in the parlor, and why he managed to seat himself beside her, on the love seat, again. As if he had any right to be jealous, possessive or otherwise attached to Arden Leigh.

He did it anyway. At least she distracted him from that sense of the sword's nearness.

Sibyl, in the meantime, seemed even more comfortable with Greta than she felt with Trace. Sinking onto the floor near Trace's feet, busying both of her slim young hands petting the cocker spaniel, she considered their pleas for the information she—as Vox07—had promised. "Don't know what to say that y'all don't already know."

More threats to out them. Great.

Arden's bare arm brushed Smith's as she leaned forward encouragingly. "All we really know is that it's a secret society, honey. A society of powerful men, who apparently turned on Greta's family in the late forties."

Oh, yeah. Greta's quest for her roots *was* what had gotten Arden involved in the first place, wasn't it? Stupid Greta.

"Leo Kaiser," agreed Sibyl, making Dido shake hands. "Exiled after World War II for challenging the society's deteriorating morality. Not the only one."

Arden asked, "What do you mean, not the only one?"

"Well, clearly," said Smith, "she means that…um…"

Sibyl scowled at him from behind her long brown hair. "Supposedly they once helped others. *Noblesse oblige.* Established in ancient times. Stewards of the people. That's why their leaders are Stuarts. From the word *steward*."

Mitch grinned. "I didn't know that! As, er…of course, none of us knew that. But, how do *you?* I mean, you're clearly not Comitatus."

Sibyl lifted Dido's ears into a bun on top of the dog's head. "Know your enemy."

Uh-oh.

"So how did the society go from helping to being villains?" asked Greta, staring out the window. Smith reminded himself that she was actively watching all of them in her peripheral vision.

"*Honores mutant mores,*" quoted Sibyl, then rolled her eyes upward at Trace's confused grunt, studying his face as she translated. "Power corrupts."

And absolute power corrupts absolutely. That sounded about right to Smith.

"You said there were others?" persisted Arden, dammit.

Again, Smith tried to steer the conversation away from the men in this room—or her father and brother. "Well, if they've been around since ancient times, there must be hundreds of thousands of others, right?"

"And other men who challenged their decline," clarified Greta, not helping.

"Sons of warriors, kings and conquerors," agreed Sibyl. "Descendents of Troy and Aeneas, of Charlemagne and El Cid and King Arthur, of Beowulf and Siegfried and Samson and Genghis Khan—"

"We get it," Smith said. "Heroes."

"Genghis Khan?" questioned Mitch, sotto voce, but Sibyl ignored him.

"Renaissance brought religious schisms. Nineteenth-century corruptions flourished. And true heroic bloodlines thinned, forgotten. Real heroes refused to participate, exiled."

Like us.

"Now," finished Sibyl darkly, "what's left is all bad."

"Stuck-up rich kids with God complexes," Trace agreed, and shared a grin down at their little narrator.

Jerk. Arden wasn't the only one of them with family still in the society. Smith's father, with whom he hadn't spoken for over a year, still was. Mitch's father and grandfather, too. Trace's—well, Trace hated his birth father, so that didn't count. He knew full well Mitch and Smith couldn't defend themselves out loud.

To Smith's surprise, Arden slid her hand into his—looking for comfort, or giving it? Like he cared? He squeezed it gently.

She squeezed back—and everything in him stilled. He slid a curious, hopeful gaze toward her—and thought he detected a faint blush staining her poise as she noted that, "Growing up rich doesn't automatically make a person corrupt. Many wealthy people have established incredible charities, used their riches to do good. And some—some are willing to sacrifice a great deal…."

God, he wished she'd look at him.

"*Honores mutant mores,*" repeated Sibyl darkly.

And Mitch, glancing out the window, said, "Not to interrupt, folks, but there's an example of one of Sib's mutants out there right now."

Much as he hated to draw his hand from Arden's, Smith stood and positioned himself beside the window so as not to draw too much attention to their discovery. He recognized the dark sedan parked down the street as easily as had Mitch. Someone didn't much value his tire pressure, did he?

"Prescott Lowell," he groaned.

And Sibyl let out a strangled gasp of betrayal.

Arden barely recognized the girl's cry, into the bare knees she'd drawn up to her face, as human. Poor thing! Immediately she fell to her knees beside Sibyl, tried to draw the girl into her arms—but the teenager twisted away from her and turned her face into Trace's legs, as if hanging on to the biggest man there would protect her. "Shouldn't have come. Shouldn't have come. Shouldn't have come."

"Great," muttered Trace. "Why's it gotta be me?"

"*Comfort her,*" snarled Arden.

Obediently, he reached down and awkwardly patted her head twice, like he might Dido, who was snuffling the girl's face with concern. Then he seemed to tire of that and pulled her hair instead. "Hey, grow up."

Arden would have chided his heartlessness—if Sibyl hadn't drawn her face out of his knees to glare up at him. "I *am* grown. And *trapped,* you idiot."

"Don't call me that!"

Arden still didn't like it, but what worked…worked.

"Don't worry, dear." Greta stood, wiped her hands on her apron. "You're welcome to stay as long as it takes for the boys to rid us of that annoyance. Again."

Sibyl nodded and murmured, "Safety in numbers. Enemy of my enemy…"

Arden, relieved of that concern, went to Smith's side. She liked being at Smith's side. It felt…right. Right, after far too much wrong. "Let's just call the police and report him for harassment."

Smith eyed her, as if torn about disagreeing—which wasn't like him—but it was Sibyl, behind them, who said, "Comitatus own the police. And the courts."

The sheer powerlessness the girl felt against this secret society was too much for Arden. "My father still has some clout in this town, as well."

"Can't disagree," muttered the girl.

Arden looked at the others, who were acting as if this man in his car was some kind of monster. He wasn't. Comitatus or not, he was just a man. That society of his couldn't remain secret if enough people asked questions. They couldn't treat people the way they had Greta's father—or, Arden truly suspected, Smith and Mitch—if enough people protested their pretense of omnipotence. She had no intention of giving up her personal power today, damn the consequences.

"Fine," she said—and left the house before even Smith, with a gasped *"Arden!"* could follow her.

The early evening heat of August surrounded Arden like a hot blanket as she strode, quite alone, to the car parked down the street. It was running—likely to keep the air-conditioning on—but so well-designed that its idling engine was nearly silent.

She tapped on the window, folded her arms and waited.

Nothing happened. Down the street, a knot of boys continued to play basketball on a cracked driveway. Some blocks away, a police siren sounded—not an unusual event, and nothing for concern. Despite the setting sun, which turned the western horizon a mixture of pinks, blues and oranges, the heat hadn't lessened.

Arden knocked with more force. "Prescott Lowell?"

Finally, with a waft of cold air, the driver's side window slid soundlessly down to reveal his expensive haircut, expensive smirk and gaze of absolute disdain. Only for a moment did a rush of upset, a memory from the other night, tighten her throat at his thuggish face.

Then he spoke, and the moment passed. "I figured you'd come back here. Like a rat going back to its nest."

"I don't believe we've been properly introduced," she said, her drawl thickening around the words of common courtesy. "I'm Arden Leigh, daughter of Donaldson Leigh? You crashed my daddy's party and threatened me with a knife last week. How do you do?"

"I didn't crash. I was invited."

"Not by me, and it was my party."

"At your 'daddy's' house."

"You're saying my daddy invited you?" For a moment, in the stillness between them, possibilities threatened like a looming tsunami—but he blinked first, looked down, shook his head.

As if her father made a habit of inviting his employees to expensive fundraising evenings. She should have known this man would lie. It made asking the next question feel somewhat futile, but she had to. "Why are you stalking me?"

That's when she noticed, in her periphery, a subtle movement. Even before she placed it, she felt herself relaxing in a very real way.

Smith crouched behind the car, hidden but waiting to spring to her defense if she needed it. The sense of safety in his nearness warmed her, relaxed her—and at last, maybe for the first time since he'd reappeared in her life, she didn't fight her pleasure at his nearness.

In the meantime, Lowell made self-important noises about having no interest in her beyond her involvement "in matters that don't concern you."

"Comitatus matters," she clarified, just to watch his face turn red.

"I told you," he warned through gritted teeth, "never to mention that again. Do you have a death wish?"

At least he hadn't grabbed his knife, which she saw lying ready on his passenger seat, as deadly as ever. "No, I have an information wish. Who else is in this secret society of yours? Why are they interested in me or the state comptroller? What do you think to accomplish by stalking and threatening me? Just a few questions like that."

"Why are *you* fraternizing with the likes of Smith Donnell and his crew? What do *you* hope to accomplish?"

"Why do you care? Because they aren't under your control?" Only with effort did Arden bite back the word *anymore?*

If Smith *were* a former Comitatus member, he'd taken a blood vow of secrecy. She didn't want to imply that he'd broken it, even if she wished he had.

For her.

"You just keep asking questions, sugar," Lowell sneered. "And talk loudly for the microphone, okay?"

And he held up his cell phone—which apparently had a record feature.

Arden showed her dimples and started to ask, "Is that supposed to worry me?"

But it must have worried Smith, because she only got out "Is that—" before he'd sprung from behind the car and pushed between her and Lowell. Arden stumbled against the curb, barely keeping her balance, while Smith tried to launch himself through the open window with a snarled, "Give me that!"

"Like hell, traitor!"

With a screech of tires, the sedan tore away from the curb—with Smith still hanging on. It zigzagged wildly as its driver struggled to retain possession of the phone. For a moment, Arden thought Smith would triumph. He *should* triumph. He was her hero.

And a reckless idiot. But perhaps he could be both.

As the sedan picked up speed, all she cared about was him surviving the battle. His feet were still on the pavement, unable to run fast enough to keep up. In a moment he was hanging on to the door even as the car straightened, even as the window began to slide shut.

Arden began to run after them.

"You son of a—!" She could hear his furious insult—the whole block could—before Smith lost his hold on the speeding sedan and hit the street. Bounced. Rolled.

And lay horribly still.

Chapter 10

"Smith!" It seemed to take forever for her to even reach him, to drop to her knees on the burning black asphalt. She drew his head into her skirted lap, then feared that he might have hurt his back, then accepted that it was too late to *not* move him and could only pray. She petted hair away from his face and saw a spatter of blood, more than road burn could explain. Quickly she began to run her hands over him and found a glaze of blood spilling from a hash of cuts on both forearms.

Didn't television cop shows call those defensive wounds? Lowell had had his knife with him, after all.

She pressed a lace-trimmed handkerchief against the worst of his arms, hated feeling so helpless. Should she move him further? Should she call an ambulance? To her relief, Smith's brown eyes opened on his own accord, and he even had the gall to grin at her, even if his grin was part wince.

"You should see the other guy," he assured her, and groaned.

Her hero, all right. She gently slapped his shoulder with her free hand. "You son of a bitch!"

Smith's eyes widened. "Ard?"

"How could you do something so stupid? And over a *cellphone recording?*"

"Well, I had to try."

She rose up on her knees, so that he slid off her lap and back onto the concrete with a murmured, "Ow."

"No, you did not have to try. You did not have to risk your life or your anonymity. Lowell can't be that dangerous."

"Actually…" Levering himself up into a sitting position with one bloodied arm, Smith glanced meaningfully at the stained lace on the other.

"Daddy can protect me," Arden insisted. "Val can protect me. I can protect myself and, clearly, *you* can protect me, but not if he kills you!"

"I wouldn't let him kill—" But then Smith threw himself against her, a hand grabbing the back of her head, pulling her face into his shirt, protecting her as he rolled once, twice, again. Hot pebbles dug into her bare arms. Unable to see, Arden flinched from the sound of a racing motor, a crash of glass, a squeal of tires.

Only as Smith's death grip on her lessened, in the shelter of a wheel-less pickup truck sitting against the curb, did Arden realize what had happened. Prescott Lowell had come back around the corner and tried to run them down as Smith lay in the street.

Smith's friend Trace had intercepted him, man against machine, with a crowbar to the windshield.

Now Trace stalked behind the black car and, in one swing, took out its rear windshield, as well. He was moving toward the driver's side when Lowell wisely sped away. Not a minute later, a familiar, primer-gray sedan slowed as it cruised by, long enough for Mitch to call, "*I* lose *him*. He doesn't lose me."

Then both cars vanished down the streets of Oak Cliff, and Smith and Arden remained seated, forgotten arms loose around each other, legs entangled, against the curb.

"I think I see why they're your friends," Arden said—or tried to. Her words came out more of a breathless murmur.

Instead of answering, Smith dropped his head onto her shoulder and breathed her in, muttering something over and over. When Arden tipped her ear against his thick, warm hair, she could make it out. "Dammit. Dammit. *Dammit.*"

She couldn't help it. She laughed. "We survived, didn't we? I call this a win. Except for your poor arms…."

She could feel dampness against her back where his cut arms must be bleeding through her dress. It wasn't an expensive dress—for her. For someone in a different income bracket, it would be. She didn't care.

When Smith drew back, his expression was as fierce as the voice that tore from his throat. "Lowell has you on tape, Ard."

She waited for further explanation.

"Lowell has you on tape, clearly aware of the Comitatus, asking *questions* about them. About their interest in the comptroller. About who else is involved. Once the society elders hear it… Do you have any idea how much danger you're in? How much—"

He was interrupted by his friend Trace, towering over them, offering a hand to help them up. Between Trace's big hand around hers, drawing her easily to her feet, and Smith's hands on her hips, pushing from below, their helpfulness nearly tossed Arden into the air.

"You're bleeding!" Smith scrambled to his feet before Trace could help him, using the pickup truck to brace himself, wincing from some inner pain. "Arden, God!"

Arden looked down at herself. Her elbows were barely scraped from their roll across the asphalt. She was not bleeding. "That's *your* blood, Smith. Let's get you inside. Come on."

Smith may or may not have been ready to protest that he could walk on his own, but when she lifted his arm over her shoulder and snuggled him close to her side, her own arm tight around him, he seemed to rethink that. In fact, he leaned a little into her bosom as they walked back to the house.

She suspected that was on purpose.

She didn't mind. In fact, she thoroughly enjoyed the close warmth and press of their bodies. Despite the insult to her independence, Smith's determination to protect her was hardly a negative. He'd claimed, back in her bedroom, that he hadn't wanted to break up with her. He'd said it was the biggest regret of his life.

The fact that he was beaten and bleeding from trying to protect her added an amazing truth to those statements. And remembering him in her room, and how they'd kissed… remembering how he'd kissed her to shut her up in the restaurant just today…remembering how easily Mitch had assumed they were back together…

Arden began to understand why she had not corrected Mitch.

She'd begun to assume the same thing. Worse, she *wanted* to assume it. She desperately, desperately wanted this man whom she held so close to be the hero she had once imagined he could be.

He was the one who'd broken her heart.

Maybe he was the only one who could mend it.

But as much as she wanted to luxuriate in the weight of him, the feel of his body against hers—as much as she wanted to coo over his injuries while she helped tend to them— something else niggled at the edge of Arden's concern.

It wasn't the danger to herself. "Why *are* the Comitatus interested in the state comptroller?"

Smith had been so blissfully distracted by Arden's softness, and concern and magnolia scent—distractions so powerful, he almost forgot the sword still waiting, humming, downstairs—that it took a moment for her question to break the fog.

Long enough for Trace to try answering it instead. "*What* state comptroller?"

Yeah. Trace wasn't exactly their mastermind.

Not that Smith did much better when he simply lifted one of his bleeding arms, tried to look especially injured, and said, "Ow." But at least that distracted Arden—and Greta, as soon as they got inside—long enough to figure out a better response. After all, there had been a good reason he and the others were at Arden's party for gubernatorial candidate Molly Johannes not a full week earlier.

The information they'd stolen that night had yielded some fascinating insight into the plans of the central southwest inner circle of the Comitatus.

As Smith had half suspected, they were only pretending to support the state comptroller for the governor's race. That way, they'd look particularly innocent when her campaign was ambushed by the ugliest smear tactics Smith and his friends had ever seen. If they could just gather a bit more evidence, that evidence could easily prove the society's *un*doing, as well. But obtaining that evidence…

Distractions didn't get much better, on Smith's end, than Arden tending to his wounds, even if he had to sit on a closed toilet to receive them. Her matter-of-fact manner about his blood, and the mess of her pretty pink dress, impressed him as much as her beauty ever had. She cleaned and disinfected the wounds that Lowell's ceremonial knife had left, suggested he get stitches. When Smith refused—medical facilities being firmly *on* the grid—she quietly secured them with butterfly bandages and a wound adhesive that Trace dug from his duffel bag. She waited until she was wrapping the second forearm with gauze bandage, giving Smith the appearance of wearing white gauntlets, before she again asked, "Why are the Comitatus interested in the state comptroller?"

And dammit, Smith had been so distracted by her firm, gentle touch and his fantasies about her kissing him to make him well that he didn't have any better answer than he had last time. Not without giving away stupid secrets which he had stupidly sworn to stupidly keep silent.

But this time, Sibyl was there. The teenager had watched the entire first-aid process from a quiet perch on the bathroom counter with an almost morbid fascination, her knees pulled up under her chin. Now she piped in to say, "The Comitatus are taking her down."

Smith blinked at Trace, who'd filled the doorway with a more casual interest in Smith's blood. Arden was so busy turning to stare at the teenager that she didn't seem to notice. "They *what?*"

Apparently, neither Trace nor Smith had to divulge any Comitatus secrets. Apparently, this Sibyl informant was the real thing.

"The local Comitatus have been encouraging Molly Johannes's race as a warning to women politicians," she insisted, in a complete sentence even. "Couldn't take her down as comptroller. Nobody outside politics would notice for long. What do comptrollers even do?"

"They…comptrol?" tried Trace.

Arden rolled her eyes. "The comptroller is in charge of the state's finances! That's hardly a minor position."

Sibyl leaned her cheek on her bare knees. "Yes, but we know politics. Ask the average supermarket shopper. But governor? Could become president. People notice."

Arden rose from where she'd crouched beside Smith for his ministrations. He missed her nearness. "What about Governor Ann Richards?"

"Mistake." Sibyl frowned in concentration. "On the Comitatus end. Even they couldn't elect her opponent. Not all powerful." She glared at Smith. "Just like to think so."

"Who cares what the comptroller does?" he challenged back.

"Exactly," said Sibyl.

"I mean, just now *I* don't care." When Arden turned a look of dismay on him, Smith tried another change of subject. "And how would you even know about Comitatus plans?"

"Hacked into their computers. Can we have chicken now?"

Apparently, as Trace had predicted, Greta had invited the girl to dinner.

For once, it was Arden not putting the requests of a guest first. "Not quite yet, honey."

"What exactly *do* the Comitatus have planned?" Smith clarified. Did her intel match the information he and his friends had taken out of Donaldson Leigh's office on the night of Arden's party?

Sibyl narrowed her eyes at him, as if she *knew* he knew, which annoyed him. He *did* know, but not because he was Comitatus.

Smith glared back, wishing she would get over her suspicions, stop her silent threats to tell Arden everything and just help them.

Luckily, Arden broke into the stare-off with a soft hand on his shoulder. "We have to know, in order to warn Molly."

"Smears about orgies," Sibyl offered. "Stolen state funds. Molested children she babysat. Helped at the youth center to seduce more victims." At Arden's increasing dismay, she added, "The Comitatus pay people to be witnesses, like the government did in the Lincoln conspiracy. And the MLK assassination. Giving them scripts and payoffs. I've seen the accounts."

That was much more than Smith and his band of exiles had gotten. "As in, their accounts of the supposed thefts and affairs?"

Sibyl rolled her eyes. No. She really meant the monetary accounts.

"Is it something the press will believe?" asked Arden. "Something that would hold up in court?"

"Illegal downloads off nameless computers. Comitatus owns the press." Sibyl glanced at Trace, then looked quickly away and shrugged. "And the courts."

"Not all of them," Smith insisted. Then for Arden's sake, he added, "I'd imagine."

Concern haunted Arden's pretty green eyes. "Then how do we warn Molly?"

"We don't." At her expression of betrayal, Smith stood to clarify. "Not yet. We get better proof. Irrevocable proof. Enough…" Oh God. He'd been wrestling with this decision for months.

But today, he'd seen how far the Comitatus, in the form of Prescott Lowell, was willing to go. Today, they'd set their sights on Arden.

That made the decision far easier than he'd ever expected, vows and bloodlines aside.

Proof. "Enough to take them down."

Sibyl's slumped posture straightened with real interest. Trace, who'd been arguing on the take-them-down side since their exile, grinned with anticipation. Arden looked up at Smith as if he really were her hero, which he seriously enjoyed.

Then his cell phone, in his jeans pocket, rang—and he couldn't get at it without messing up his bandage-gauntlets. Making a face, he had to lean away to offer his hip to Arden, looking hopeful.

He seriously enjoyed her retrieving his cell phone for him, too.

"It's Mitch," she said, opening it for him.

And from the hallway, hidden behind Trace, Greta Kaiser said, "You *can't* take down the Comitatus. You have to save them.

"We need heroes."

* * *

Greta could not possibly have imagined, mere weeks ago, how her simple request of Arden would change her life. Not a week ago she'd been living a lonely life of long, shadowy days and longer, silent nights. Between near blindness, near poverty and advancing age, she'd had little more than her beloved dog, a few visits from friends and a lot of memories left.

Those memories, and the holes Papa's secrecy had left in them, had meant everything. Hence her request that Arden confirm them.

But now!

Now she could barely hear over the din of her crowded kitchen table…and she loved it even more than did her happy cocker spaniel.

"The Comitatus think they can tell everyone what to do just because of their money," Trace Beaudry argued through a mouthful of mashed potatoes. "No offense."

Arden sat straighter. "No offense to whom?"

In answer, Trace grabbed another biscuit and took a bite to muffle any possible answer.

Greta wished she could see their expressions, but even their body language, at the edge of her vision, spoke volumes. She felt quite sure that Smith and Mitch both were former Comitatus like her papa. Trace, she hadn't decided yet. He had neither their breeding nor their composure. But the bigger man had worked tirelessly at long-neglected repairs to her home. He treated her with unflagging respect. He was, she suspected, smarter than his impatience and social bluntness let on.

And she adored feeding so enthusiastic an eater.

"They used to be heroes," she reminded everyone, passing around the platter of fried chicken. "My father gave up everything trying to redeem them. Perhaps it's not too late. The world needs heroes."

Smith said nothing. She wished she could see his expression most of all. He seemed to have so much going on behind his cavalier attitude.

Arden said, "Whatever we do, can we do it in time to save Molly's reputation?"

Trace swallowed his biscuit. "Destroying them would be more fun."

Young Sibyl appeared to nod enthusiastically.

"I'm not especially worried about the comptroller," Smith admitted finally. "I'm worried about Arden."

"Nobody asked you to be," the recipient of his worry challenged.

"They've got you on tape. Greta will be safer if you're not here. Mitch should be back soon." But Smith turned toward the cuckoo clock on Greta's kitchen wall. "He can help Trace watch Greta's place."

"Which reminds me—where is Mitch?" asked Arden.

Sibyl said, "I can help Trace protect Greta."

Trace snickered. The others stared.

"Thank you, dear." Greta offered Sibyl more green beans. Whatever her story was, she obviously felt safer here, too.

Just as Greta did, now that the young folks were around.

Arden asked again, "Where *is* Mitch? Is he all right?"

"He's fine," Smith insisted. "But he couldn't stop Lowell, so you're going to have to stay away from your usual haunts for a few days. No going back to your apartment, or your father's place or the rec center."

That would not sit well. "Smith, the youth center is my life."

"It could *lose* you your life if the Comitatus find you there."

"And how long do you see me staying in hiding?"

"Until we stop them."

"Then let's stop them. And, oh, yes, *where is Mitch?* Where did he follow Lowell?"

After a long, stretched silence, Smith admitted, "Local Comitatus headquarters."

"Where's that?" asked Trace, then startled. "Ouch!"

Arden sat back in her chair. "Smith, did you just *kick him?*"

It was time to put a stop to this. "I called Valeria while you were tending to Smith's wounds," Greta admitted. "She'll be here soon to watch out for me, so that nobody else need feel obliged. Arden, she says you can stay at her apartment tonight. I doubt anyone will look for you there. Does that settle everything?"

"No," Smith and Arden grumped at the same time and turned to each other, likely startled by their mutual reaction. As if they weren't meant for each other.

It was amazing, thought Greta, how much she could see with these old, failing eyes that they could not. She only hoped her need of their help wasn't putting any of them into worse danger.

No amount of improvements to her life would be worth that.

Arden felt her blood starting to boil yet again. She'd been more than patient. She'd been willing to wait until they had some privacy to ask Smith about his involvement with the Comitatus. But if Smith was going to behave like a child, all bets were off.

Considering the feelings this day had released in her, feelings she'd thought lost—admiration, attraction, more—the idea of private time held more danger than simply learning a hard-to-imagine truth. But what did *he* have to be grumpy about? He was the one keeping secrets about Mitch, kicking Trace under the table, trying to keep her ignorant about everything.

If it was just to protect her, Arden feared she might show him just how little she needed his protection. She might show him with some kind of blunt object. It wasn't as if the day's adventure hadn't soiled and stained her sundress beyond redemption.

"We've still got to worry about our little conspiracy theorist here," Smith scowled. "And who's going to keep an eye on Arden at Val's?"

Trace snorted. "Yeah. Big mystery. Who gets to guard Arden's body— *Stop it!*"

At least *that* kick didn't need explaining.

"And what are we going to do about Molly?" demanded Arden.

"It's being taken care of," insisted Mr. Mystery, as if that would appease her.

"And the Comitatus?"

"Ditto."

She narrowed her eyes. "And I'm supposed to do what— hide and look pretty?"

Smith narrowed his eyes right back at her. "The looking pretty is optional."

"It's the hiding part I don't like."

"Why? Is it in poor taste?"

Things degenerated from there. Luckily, Val soon arrived to interrupt the escalation of World War III—to the apparent disappointment of Trace and Sibyl, who'd been eating home-baked cookies as they watched, like refreshments at a sports competition. Arden's friend strode into Greta's house, looking wholly in charge and ready to take on anything that might threaten the older woman.

Even Dido, though still excited for the company, didn't bark at Val.

"Take my car," Val murmured simply to Arden, pressing a key chain into her hand, then lowered her voice to a husky whisper. "There's protection in the bedside table."

Then, only a gleam in her topaz eyes to indicate her amusement, Val continued on to meet the mysterious Vox07, aka Sibyl.

Arden stared momentarily at the keys in her hand. *Protection…?*

For a moment she thought Val meant she'd left a second gun. Then she realized… But that was ridiculous, right?

"Are you ready to go?" demanded Smith from the door-way, in a voice she would moments ago have labeled as petulant. "Or do you have to fix your hair or something?"

But Arden suddenly suspected that his petulance and bad humor were as much a protective mask as some of his smiles. Because, with a hollow swoop deep inside her where she'd been guarding her heart, she suddenly realized that hers certainly were.

Protective.

A mask.

She wasn't furious at Smith at all.

She just hadn't wanted to admit, even to herself, how badly she needed to take him to bed.

Arden was strangely quiet as she drove Smith to her friend Valeria's apartment. Smith wouldn't blame her if she was still angry. Angry, he could handle. But—*silent?*

That, thought Smith grimly, was not going to make this easy.

They were supposed to fight, dammit. He would keep sniping at her until she dropped that challenging, überpolite front of hers and sniped back. Her temper would then hold him back the way her vague pleasantries had no hope of doing. Eventually there would be yelling and, if he was lucky, slamming doors, and it wouldn't matter how much he still needed her.

It wouldn't matter how every bit of air had left his body when she'd stalked outside to face down Prescott Lowell.

It wouldn't matter how protective rage had blinded him when he'd realized the damaging proof Lowell had gotten on her. It wouldn't matter how he'd felt when she'd knelt over him in the road, her eyes glistening with concern and dismay over his injuries, or how she'd felt in his arms as he'd rolled them out of the way of the car, or how gently she'd tended his wounds at Greta's place.

Yelling and slammed doors. That should do the trick of

keeping them apart. Sniping and keeping them safe. But she wasn't cooperating.

Did he have to handle *everything*?

As soon as they'd locked themselves into Valeria Diaz's second-floor apartment, in a small complex old enough to boast large floor plans and tiny kitchen units, Smith channeled his frustration into yet another volley. "This has been a crappy day. If you think I'm sleeping on the floor just because you're the lady, you have another—"

But Arden's sudden kiss stole the rest of the challenge right out of his mouth.

Chapter 11

The hell with argument.

Smith kissed her back.

He slid the fingers of one hand into her thick, black hair, tasted the curve and sweetness of her lips, used his other arm to brace against the small of her back as he held her as safe as he could, as close to him as he could, and kissed her until he felt dizzy from lack of oxygen, or rapid heart rate…or love.

She was marvelous, exquisite. And for this moment she was his, his, his….

Something poked at the back of his mind, and he ignored it to kiss Arden.

Her soft arms looped smoothly behind his neck, hanging on to him as if for life. She sank against him, her breasts pillowing erotically against his chest, her cheek resting on his shoulder as he turned his head to follow her lips. He'd wanted this for so long, wanted her.…

Of everything he'd lost in his exile from the Comitatus, from his previous life, the loss of Arden really had been the worst.

You're still exiled, the little voice poked. *You're still dirt-poor. You still don't deserve her.*

And even worse—you've got other duties.

But she was still kissing him, so he had no trouble shutting out that voice with the louder one—*She's gorgeous, fearless, perfect. I could have lost her. It's been so damned long….*

When she turned her face away, into his shoulder to catch her breath, he took advantage of the moment to gulp some much needed air of his own and said nothing. He just savored her cuddling against him, so close, so beautiful, and he refused to be the one to draw back again. He didn't want to draw back, ever. He never had wanted that.

With him stoically saying nothing, it was her who looked up and said, "Take me to the bedroom."

Smith almost winced in expected disappointment before the words registered. She didn't think this was a mistake? She wasn't asking for more gentlemanly treatment? What about her six-month rule?

Who cared? He scooped her and all her dirt-stained pink skirtage up into his arms, barely noticing the twinge from his bandaged cuts. Arden gasped and then laughed, husky and erotic, as he carried her in the direction that the bedroom should be. Back hallway, good. A door—

"Not that one." Arden laughed as he pushed it open with his foot. Ah. Tiny bathroom.

He grunted manfully, followed her graceful point, and pushed through the other door into a large bedroom with brick-red walls and rustic, oversized furniture. He deposited Arden on the bed, then hopped eagerly aboard himself, rolling into a position over her, taking his weight on his knees and elbows to kiss her more thoroughly.

She all but purred as her soft body stretched out and shifted beneath him.

It wasn't long before he was starting to do some writhing himself. It wasn't much longer before he was kissing across the collar of her dress, sliding a hand up under her skirt to savor the delicacy of her skin, bearing down on her—just a little—to test his welcome through his jeans.

The way she moved against him, she didn't seem the least bit unwelcoming. Until—

"Up," she demanded, probably more than once since he was having trouble hearing her through the rush in his ears. When he placed her command, he reluctantly sank back, off of her, and sat up on his knees. She slid her legs under her on the bed, as well—

And surprised him again by grabbing the bottom of his T-shirt and tugging it upward.

Damn—was this even Arden, or had Smith hit his head when he lost his grip on Lowell's car? If this was just an erotic dream, he hoped he could dream it to the end. He obediently stripped his shirt up and over his head and, at her insistence, let her ease the sleeves more carefully over his bandage-gauntlets. She was barely done before he was scooping billows of her own rosy sundress up and over her head, revealing soft scoops of flesh supported by the a red lace bra....

Finally, words tugged out of him. "You were *planning* this?"

She shook her head with a smile that somehow managed to be both knowing and innocent. "If a lady knows she's well put together under her clothes, she's more likely to—"

Got it. He laid her back on the bed and resumed the kissing of her, starting with the edge of that bra.

Some part of him repeated *She wasn't planning this, either.* As if that meant something. But as long as it meant they were finally going to make love, finally going to consummate the deep connection they'd felt, then fought, then danced around for so long, he wasn't about to question it. Instead he murmured, when he could find words, how beautiful she was, how perfect she was, how badly he'd missed her.

Her hands massaged his scalp through his hair, and the back of his neck and his shoulders. She kissed his jaw, kissed down his neck, kissed across his chest. And she murmured, "Oh, Smith, I do love you…."

At least once. When he finally heard it—

That's when he rolled off her.

Dammit! Dammit, dammit, dammit. No matter how badly he'd been living for over a year. No matter how rebellious he'd been in his youth. No matter how much he loved flaunting the rules. Some part of him needed to be the gentleman that she wanted, the hero that she deserved, badly enough to stop.

"Smith?" She slid a hand down his bare chest, toward his jeans, but he caught her wrist and—in pain from more than his injuries—asked, "But what about your six-month rule?"

Her smile lit the shadowy room. "Let's call it retroactive." Dark hair curling heavily down to curtain them to either side, she leaned over him, kissed him.

He kissed her back at first—but didn't let go of her wrist. *Duty, dammit.* As soon as he'd summoned a little more willpower, he said, "I may not be around much longer, Ard. Not if my plans against—not if I manage everything I've been working toward."

This time he saw the flash of pain in her beautiful green eyes. But, stubbornly, simply, she said, "Then let's make the most of the time we have."

When she bent to kiss him, he set his mouth, seriously unsettled. *She loved him.*

She deserved better.

She drew back and said, "It's all right if you don't love me back—" That's when he rolled completely off the bed and to his bare feet.

"What kind of crap is *that?*"

"Smith?" There she knelt, her chest heaving against that incredible bra, her slip askew enough to show a hint of matching red lace on one luscious hip, in the middle of Valeria Diaz's now-rumpled bed. And here he stood, shirtless and barefoot and barely able to think through his hard, throbbing need of her. And *it didn't matter if he didn't love her?*

"Of course it matters!" Smith argued, channeling all his frustration out into his words. "Don't you ever say—much less do this with any— I mean…"

Okay, way to ruin a good tirade. That was the problem with letting his frustration talk.

Her gaze searched his, trying to make sense of him, so he went with the most simple, most undeniable of his truths. "I love you, too, dammit."

Which did nothing to help the fact that a relationship between them was near about impossible, as long as her father was head of the Comitatus, as long as Smith was blacklisted from getting any solid job or even a decent apartment. It did nothing to help the fact that he'd kept secrets from her, from the moment they'd met, and that he was still keeping them. It did nothing to help the way his secrets could tear her family— not just her father, but her baby brother—from her in raw wounds that might never heal.

But words couldn't be spoken to help any of that. And the other words…

They were so easy to say that he tried them again. "No matter what else happens, Arden Leigh, I love you with everything I've got left. So don't you dare say it doesn't matter. It matters. *You* matter. You always have mattered."

She gazed at him, seeming to measure his words. They'd known each other, maybe loved each other, for years, and yet somehow this was the first time they'd dropped every protective facade.

The first time they'd really stopped sparring.

After a moment of silence, Arden twisted on the bed just enough to draw her ruffly slip off her hips and butt—the red lace panties were even better than the bra—and down her smooth, pale thighs and off her curved, firm calves. She dropped them off the side of the bed and sat there like some kind of virgin sacrifice. Like a bride on her wedding night.

Like a goddess.

"Smith," she said softly. "Darling Smith. Come to bed."

Don't touch her, whispered a rapidly fading warning from somewhere inside him. *If you touch her, you'll be lost.*

But he both loved her and needed her so badly that he stripped off his jeans and did just that.

Arden woke to late morning light, stretched in the unconscious loop of Smith's heavy arms, and felt loved. Thoroughly. Physically. Emotionally.

Smith loved her.

From what she could read between the lines, between his sighs and his kisses, he'd loved her even when he'd broken up with her.

Broken up with her because he was—had been—part of a powerful, all-male secret society that had turned bad.

She wasn't quite sure what she felt about that, beyond one determined certainty: Smith was one of the good guys.

No matter what else she knew or did not know, she believed that with every cell in her body.

She watched him sleep, noting how his face relaxed in unconsciousness, no smiling mask of biting humor, no scowl of self-protective disapproval. His beauty went deeper than cheekbones, stubbly jaw, or that slightly crooked nose. It was the face of a man who had sacrificed not just for the good, but for her. Who was still sacrificing for her.

She felt approval stretch her lips into a smile. *Her hero.*

And to think that, even before their first breakup, she'd thought him more of an antihero.

He also had a smear of something brown on his chest, which looked oddly like a…handprint. The size of her hand. Carefully, so as to not wake him, Arden freed her hands and arms enough to see the random brown smudging here and there on her skin. She sniffed one, and her stomach turned far more from the significance than the faintly rusty smell.

Blood.

He must have opened one of his wounds during their second bout of lovemaking.

Remembering how he'd drawn back after smudging her with dust, back in her bedroom, Arden did her best to slide backward out of bed without waking him.

"Hey," he murmured, his fingers tightening on the small of her back. "You okay? You're still here?"

So she kissed him. Any excuse to kiss him. "Powder-room break. I'll be right back."

To her relief, he didn't open his eyes. "Promise?"

"Promise."

With a deep, sleepy sigh, he turned his face into the pillow and let her go. She was able to slip into the bathroom and wash the smears of dried blood off herself before he could see them. She considered combing her hair, which was a woolly mess, but decided that she preferred the honesty of it, of the whisker burn flushing one cheek, of the spattering of freckles across her bare, powderless nose. Instead, she simply wrapped herself in Val's boldly striped cotton robe before finding her friend's first-aid kit.

She carried it and several dark towels back to the bed with her.

Smith was awake—barely—and waiting for her. At her reappearance, his petulant expression eased into a more honest smile than she may ever have seen on his playful features. "Hey, there, sweetness."

"Good morning, yourself." She smiled, kneeling on the bed beside him and opening the box.

"Bandages...towels...antibacterial wipes... You like it kinky, huh?"

"Hush up and give me your arm."

He did and lay with surprising obedience, caressing her with his gaze as she cleaned and rebandaged his wounds. Warmed by his unfeigned approval, Arden was glad she hadn't combed her hair or put on makeup.

"You really should have had these seen to at a hospital," she murmured finally, wrapping the second arm.

"One of the secrets to living off the grid is avoiding places like emergency rooms." Saying that, he flinched—and not, Arden thought, because of her ministrations.

They'd more or less avoided this subject last night. He'd been trying to hide the truth from her, from the start. But if they were to have any hope—

After the miracle of their lovemaking, there had to be hope.

She took a deep breath. "You're living off the grid because of your exile from the Comitatus."

Smith said nothing, his surprisingly vulnerable brown gaze searching her face.

"I'm not a fool, Smith."

"I know that."

"And I realize—Greta said that her father took vows of secrecy. The only reason he told her anything was because of his Alzheimer's. So I imagine that if you took similar vows then, well..." She smiled wryly. "You can neither confirm nor deny."

He shrugged a hard, bare shoulder, still watching her as if counting her breaths. His eyes spoke volumes...and the helplessness of his silence soothed her as words never could. If he hadn't taken a vow of secrecy, then he full well could deny it.

In his silence, she had her answer.

She moved the first-aid kit to the bedside table so that she could scoot closer beside him. Being beside him felt *right*. "Don't worry about confessions. I just want you to know how *I* see it. I think you joined this organization because you believed in their heroic legends, the part of them Greta's still certain exists. You joined..." Of course. "Your father must belong, as well, and his father. Smith, have you even seen your parents since—since we broke up?"

Apparently, that he could answer. "I've visited my mother a couple of times, when I knew my father was out of town."

"You poor..." When she saw his eyes narrow, she remembered how little men liked to be pitied. "Your poor mother."

Again he shrugged, as if to dismiss their separation as par for the course. Considering that he'd initially dismissed their own relationship with a similar artificial indiffernce, Arden didn't believe him. But she, of anyone, understood social lies.

She thought of her own close bond with her father, tried to imagine being banished from him, and couldn't bear the thought. Guilt and discomfort closely followed her wash of relief. She didn't want to think about her father.

"In any case," she continued, "you decided to leave, accepting exile rather than...than something. I can't imagine you giving up so much, your inheritance, your status, for anything of mere surface importance. I think—I *know* that you must have left for honorable reasons. And you broke up with me to protect me from the fallout of your decision."

In a moment's thought, that part of her summary turned sour, and she punched him softly in the naked shoulder.

"Ow," protested Smith, though she doubted she'd hurt him. "Some lady *you* are."

"You broke up with me to *protect* me? That's not chivalry, Smith, that's chauvinism. How dare you presume to know what's best for someone else?"

Smith opened his mouth as if to respond and then, just as firmly, closed it.

Vows of secrecy, decided Arden, were just plain tacky. "In any case," she decided, drawing fingers in a soft apology over the area she'd just hit, "you're back. And I know you might not be able to stay. I accept that. But until you have to go— don't lie to me again. Please?"

Her name broke from him. "Ard. I don't want to hurt you, but."..."

"Of course you'll have to omit things. I understand that. But at the very least—come to me and let me know you're leaving. You don't have to say why. But don't pretend you don't love me. Knowing that you love—"

He silenced the rest of her plea with a kiss, wrapping his freshly bandaged arms tightly behind her. "I promise," he assured her, his voice rough with truth. "I promise, Arden. I promise."

And that—that had to be enough.

For now.

Chapter 12

Smith had never felt so content, so right, so damned lucky in his life.

By his estimate, that meant something would *definitely* be going wrong very soon.

Leaving Arden even for a while felt like a sacrifice, like a tie between them was being pulled tighter and tighter as he caught a city bus back to Greta's neighborhood. But he had duties. Sort of. Arden had been adamant about changing the bedclothes and, while she was at it, doing an extra load of laundry for their hostess. And people like Lowell were less likely to find her at Val's than at Greta's, which was rapidly becoming some kind of Home for the Formerly Comitatus.

Today it was Val Diaz who blocked Smith's entrance into the old Victorian, her tawny arms folded, her legs set and her expression no-nonsense. "How's Arden?"

Arden was brilliant. Arden was perfect. Arden was everything Smith had ever wanted in life, even before he'd known he wanted it. The way she'd looked at him after their goodbye kiss at the door, before he forced himself away to take care of those pesky little details about everyone's safety, betraying cabals and stopping the campaign against Molly Johannes… Well, he'd almost left everyone, from gubernatorial candidates to blind old ladies, to their own devices. Except…

Well, part of how she'd looked at him made him feel strangely, sappily heroic. *She* thought he was honorable, and her belief that he was a good guy did more to bolster his own faith in that possibility than any number of Comitatus-styled power plays could. He didn't want to shatter her faith in him. So…here he was. Back within that humming awareness of the hidden Comitatus sword.

And he wasn't about to say any of that to Val. "I let her sleep in. She's safer at your place."

Val grunted, her meaning somehow both dark and in-scrutable, but let him by. At least little Dido was happy to see him, to judge by her wiggles.

Smith immediately dismissed the crazy thought that the Sword of Aeneas was happy to see him, too. He hadn't liked his dreams of fighting and founding empires—not when they included the loss of his truest love. He'd preferred waking up to Arden.

The other strays that Greta had been collecting clustered around the kitchen table—yes, the one near the secret compartment that held the sword, dammit—and another big breakfast. Smith didn't want to think about duty yet. Not if he might have to choose it over Arden. But life couldn't just stop, either. Young Sibyl still hadn't left, which vaguely worried him about possible kidnapping charges on their part. But she looked especially wary and hands-off this morning, so Smith said nothing. Trace grunted noncommittally through the food he was eating. And Mitch had gotten back at some point, hopefully with everything Smith had requested.

"Hey, Mitch, can I borrow a shirt?" Smith grabbed a couple of sausages off the platter before they vanished like yesterday's sticky buns.

"You didn't even *change clothes?*" demanded Val with full scorn, entering the kitchen behind him.

"I showered," Smith defended. "These are new bandages. But it would've taken too long to get to our hotel room and back just for a shirt."

"Yes, you may borrow a shirt," Mitch interjected. "I have many, many clean clothes, for I am an admirably clean person."

Val rolled her eyes.

"But not in an obsessive/compulsive way," Mitch added.

Smith waited. Dido cocked her head and lifted one foot in pretty entreaty, her chocolate spaniel eyes on the sausage in Smith's fingers. *Fat chance, dog.*

Mitch stopped gazing at Val. "Oh! You'd probably like me to get said shirt. Let me show you your many, many clean options."

He headed up the back stairs, which he and Trace had apparently cleared at some point over their visit, and laughed when Smith smacked him on the back of the head for being a babbling idiot. Val wasn't *that* attractive.

At least, Smith didn't think so. Anyway, she was more Trace's type, not that Trace seemed to be saying anything to her in the silent kitchen behind them.

In any case, what he really wanted to see was the satchel of supplies Mitch had promised, during their phone call the previous night, to bring with him.

The same ones they'd taken to Arden's father's estate not a week earlier.

They'd been at Donaldson Leigh's study, infiltrating the local Comitatus, for a reason after all. In the last few days Smith, Mitch and Trace had already gone over most of what they'd found out—the stolen keystroke data, the voice recordings. That's how they'd learned about the plan against the gubernatorial candidate. To judge by all the luxury rental cars Mitch had noted gathering outside Leigh's six-car garage, the Comitatus would make their move sometime today. That meant Smith and his band of exiles had to move sooner, get film and audio of them in the act and…

And do what?

Exposing the lot of them for what they were held its own lure. While it wouldn't bring down the entire organization, from the high-and-mighty Stuarts on down, it would effectively cripple the inner circle for the central southwest. But that meant breaking their own vows of secrecy, once and for all, which would bring down far worse retribution from the society than ruined credit or social exile. They'd have a price on their heads, by people who could pay very dearly.

And it meant exposing Smith's own father.

And it meant exposing *Arden's* father—and, before leaving her for her own safety, facing her horror when she realized that the biggest secret Smith had been keeping from her wasn't about himself at all, but about her beloved father's corruption.

It also meant destroying any chance the exiles might have of doing what Greta had wanted, somehow returning the organization to its former heroic glory.

All bad things. But their other option…

Could the Comitatus somehow be blackmailed into cleaning up their act?

"These are good cameras," said Mitch, laying three of them across the bed in his small Victorian guestroom while Smith stripped off yesterday's T-shirt.

Smith was careful of his bandaged forearms as he shrugged his arms into one of Mitch's white guayabera button-downs with brown embroidery running in two stripes down the front. It was that or pastel—yellow, or pink or blue—and those had embroidery, as well. Mitch already wore the mossy green.

No accounting for taste.

"If we can just set them up before the meeting, we've got a shot at some excellent footage," Mitch continued. "But to get the best stuff…"

"We'd need to be on the inside." Smith paused in buttoning. "And that's not happening unless you've got some great hide-in-the-closet scheme that doesn't turn out like a bad sitcom."

Mitch grinned. "I say we have Trace take out the guard, then film through the window."

Smith raised both eyebrows.

"Seriously! It's not like they won't find out we were there damned soon afterward anyway. Trace would love the chance to practice being violent, and we already saw that they only post one guard—"

"Last time. But they know we're here now."

"Then *you* take out the hypothetical second guard while I film. Cleverly disguised as a shrub. Like in *Macbeth*."

"I think we should try getting the cameras in ahead of time." Which meant leaving, oh…about fifteen minutes ago. If not last night.

No way would Smith have missed last night.

"Love's making you cowardly, Donnell."

Smith glared.

"And anyway, how would we get the equipment back in? They aren't having a big party like last time. Hey!" Mitch perked up. "Maybe Arden could get us in!"

Now Smith really glared.

"Or maybe not. Maybe—"

Dido began to bark furiously downstairs, a shrill note in the dog's alarm that Smith hadn't heard when someone merely arrived at the door. Then—

"Fire!" yelled Trace from the front of the house.

"More than one," called Val from the kitchen. "We've got one back here, too!"

Smith broke for the stairs, Mitch close behind.

The scene that met them in the front foyer, even more than the sudden scorching smell of smoke, slowed Smith's step. Greta knelt on the wood floor, fumbling to fasten a leash to her beloved pet's collar while Dido spun in frantic circles. And Trace loomed as if made of stone, a throw off the sofa in his hands, glaring at the front doorway.

Where young Sibyl deliberately blocked his way out, her back against the door, her mouth opening and closing without sound, a fireplace poker in hand.

"Don't think I won't break you in half," Trace warned.

Sibyl shook her head determinedly, her dark eyes narrow behind her long, loose hair—the traitor in their midst. Her mouth opened, then closed, but she said nothing.

"I could use some help back here!" called Val from somewhere behind them.

With a quick, "I'm on it," Mitch headed that way.

Smith joined Trace in facing down Sibyl. "I knew we couldn't trust you, you crazy little—"

"Hey!" snapped Trace—at Smith!—at the same time Sibyl brandished the poker at him.

Smith took a quick step back. Okay. So calling the weird girl names wasn't the best way to fix this. Somehow, he managed to find his calm place. "Greta? Maybe you and Dido should go out the back way. And make sure someone's called nine-one-one, 'kay?"

Finally, Sibyl found her voice. "No!"

"Sorry then." But Trace wouldn't apologize unless he really was going to take her. Smith caught his friend back by the very big arm.

"This is the way you treat people who try to help you?" he challenged the girl instead. "You let them burn alive?"

"No—look! A trap!"

Smith looked. Flames, licked up the half-dead oak tree that

fronted Greta's house, seeming surreal in the August sunlight, like a special effect. But the smoke that churned off them…

Sibyl shook her head, tried again. With her free hand, she slapped the decorative window just beside the door. *"Look!"*

Trace had guts—Smith had to give him that. He stepped into poker range and looked.

And cursed. "Dark car. She's right. It's a trap to flush us out."

At that, the teenager dropped her weapon and slid down the door to kneel at their feet, relief etched across her half-hidden face. She simply nodded.

"A trap," Smith repeated. And Sibyl had figured that out. "Swell."

Trace tossed the poker well out of the young girl's reach, just in case, as he hauled her up by one arm. "Hello. Fire?"

Smith glanced out at the burning tree, searched his memory for the location of the front faucet, and happily remembered that when he'd arrived, it was already attached to a hose and sprinkler. He unholstered his revolver and handed it over. "I go out, you cover me."

"'Kay." After moving Sibyl even farther from the front door, Trace flung it open and stepped out onto the porch—gun first. Courage had never been his problem. Smith followed, praying that the sight of a large man with a Saturday Night Special aimed directly at them would keep any watching Comitatus from taking advantage of his vulnerability.

He could feel an imaginary target on his back as he hurried to the outdoor faucet, turned it on full force, unscrewed the sprinkler and began spraying the flaming oak tree. He pressed his thumb across the nozzle to create a more pressurized spray of water, focusing on the branches closest to the house.

His whole world became smoke.

Smoke stung his eyes, near blinding him. Smoke scorched his throat, his lungs. Smoke streaked his hands and arms as he sprayed, sprayed, sprayed.

Burning leaves fluttered down, curled and charred, on top of him, and he tried to brush them off.

Was Dallas County under another burn ban? Probably.

He spared time to douse the shingles of the porch. A burning branch crashed onto the front walk, and he turned back to the tree.

What the hell were Mitch and Val doing? Had Greta gotten out?

And through everything, through every choking, streaming glance Smith managed toward the dark sedan, one single thought overrode all else:

Burning out an old, blind woman?

And now they sat, just watching.

Suddenly Val Diaz was there, slapping a wet dish towel over Smith's shoulder and wrenching the hose from his stiff hands. She already wore a wet cloth over her face, like an Old West bandito. Mitch, similarly disguised, dodged past him with a wet blanket, beating at burning grass.

"Wait. What—"

"The other fire's out," Val said, muffled. "They're gone."

Smith pulled his own wet towel up over his face, dragging cool, blessed air into his scorched lungs, and looked toward the street. The sedan had left. Why—

But he knew why. A faint, distant buzz was resolving itself into sirens.

Fire trucks.

The cavalry had arrived.

Two hours later, Greta's downstairs was a mess of wet, sooty footprints, but the fires were out. The oak tree dripped wet, black drops onto the yard, charred but still remarkably alive. Mitch and Val, who looked as sooty and exhausted as Smith felt, had held back fires on Greta's garage and back porch before coming to help Smith.

"The Comitatus owns *everything*," Sibyl warned in a dire

hiss. Val, who knew several of the firefighters personally, made sure that the ones she *did* trust did the walk-through that cleared Greta's main house as safe to reenter. The arson investigator had taken copious notes and asked a lot of questions—why, yes, these fires *were* suspicious—but so far Smith and his friends had managed to avoid direct accusations.

Finally alone again—if six people and a dog could be considered "alone"—the sooty, dripping lot of them gathered around Greta's kitchen table, gulping lemonade and iced tea and tap water as fast as they could fill their glasses.

"That was a trap," announced Trace, his usually gravelly voice all the worse from the smoke.

"Ya *think?*" demanded Smith, Mitch and Val in unison.

It was Sibyl, again standing right next to Trace, who stated the harsh truth. "They can't be redeemed. They need to be stopped. All of them."

Smith glanced wearily toward Greta, the main holdout against that argument. But she, kneeling beside her dog, looked up with sadness in her vague eyes and nodded at seeming nothingness.

"They could have killed me, all of you, even Dido." Her old voice shook in regret. "Whatever was worth saving has surely changed since Papa's time. You need to stop them."

"Then we stop them." Smith's voice croaked oddly as he spoke. "Just…"

"Do not tell me you're gonna wuss out," warned Trace, standing to his impressive height. And breadth.

Like Smith would scare that easily.

"No, I am not going to wuss out. I just—I should warn Arden first. She—"

Which is when the back of his mind did the math, and something inside him froze.

"Warn Arden about what?" demanded Val, while Smith dug his prepaid cell phone from his pocket.

"That Arden's father is the head of the local Comitatus," answered Sibyl, strangely certain about even more details.

Smith stared at the display on his phone, at the *3 Missed Calls* message.

He hadn't heard his phone ring, what with all the excitement. Arden...

"Who else is in this secret society of yours?" asked Arden's sweet voice from the minirecorder in Donaldson Leigh's hand. "Why are they interested in me or the state comptroller?"

He snapped it off before the part about Smith Donnell— but they'd already heard that. Several times. Too often.

Leigh had seen tragedy in his life. Wealth and greatness hardly protected a man from losing parents, losing wives. But never, until now, had he felt true heartbreak.

Arden...

How had he raised a daughter who would so flagrantly disobey him, so willfully pursue matters that were none of her business?

"You don't have to do this." His friend Will Donnell stood very still in the corner of Leigh's otherwise-empty study.

"You're one to talk," growled Leigh, not looking up. "This is your traitor's fault."

Will did not deny that his only son had betrayed them. They'd known that for over a year—and now they had Smith on tape, too. Will's voice stayed carefully neutral. "He left my protection when he left the brotherhood. Arden..."

Leigh finally raised his eyes, hoping he could hide his pain as thoroughly as his friend. "Some would argue that she left my protection when she left home, certainly when she pursued this foolish quest and took up with...well. Now she's endangering us all. It must be stopped."

Leigh pressed the speed-dial button for his baby girl. Only the nobility born in him from generations of purebred Leighs, from a lifetime in the grand society of the Comitatus, gave him the strength to ignore the ache of loss, the bitter taste of this double betrayal.

"Thank you for calling," drawled his daughter's musical voice—also a recording. "I'm so sorry I can't pick up, but if you'll be so kind as to leave a message, I'll get back to you quick as a jackrabbit. 'Bye now!"

At the beep, he said, "Darling? It's Daddy. Jeff's hurt himself—nothing life-threatening, but his arm may be broken, and he's refusing to go to the doctor. If you get this, we surely could use your presence at home."

Then he hung up, somehow exhausted.

After a few long breaths, he met Will Donnell's stoic gaze, sharing more than most strong men could.

They waited.

Will turned suddenly toward the window, brow furrowed as if he'd seen something—but that's when the phone rang.

Arden, announced the caller-ID screen.

Leigh answered on speakerphone—because she was now a Comitatus problem, not his baby. Never again his baby. "This is Leigh."

Still, the concern in her honeyed voce wrenched his heart as she said, "Daddy?"

Chapter 13

"Come again?" demanded Val, her voice as dangerous as her expression.

Smith hardly listened to Sibyl's reiteration—that Arden's father was head of the local Comitatus—as he dialed into his voice mail.

"*Madre de Dios,*" swore Arden's friend, while a soot-darkened Mitch cocked his head to ask the teen, "Is there *nothing* you don't know?"

"Shut up," snapped Smith, at all of them.

He felt himself beginning to unravel. Oh God. Oh God, oh God, oh God. He'd left Arden almost four hours ago. Val didn't *own* that much laundry.

Where the hell was she?

Maybe the others heard something in his voice, because they shut up in time for him to hear her message.

"Hi, Smith." Her voice sounded innocent and affectionate, momentarily surrounding him with the memory of this incredible morning. "Jeff's been in a skateboarding accident—I think he'll be all right, but I'm heading out to make sure, and I don't want to waste time coming by for you if you're off somewhere else. Call me *quickly* if you want to come along. I... Well, 'bye then."

"She's going to her father's," he told the others, barely able to listen to the second message. But it could be something important.

Venom dripped from Val's words. "Good job protecting her."

And then the second message, cooler in comparison.

"I'm almost to Highland Park, so—no carpooling today after all. I know you're worried about the Comitatus sitting in wait for me, but Daddy's place is very safe—I'll turn around the moment I see anything suspicious, cross my heart."

She'd left no third message.

Smith held his breath and dialed her number. The rings lasted an eternity.

And then: "Thank you for calling. I'm so sorry I can't pick up, but if you'll be so kind as to leave a message—"

He disconnected, his heart beating like drums at an execution. This time, the tightness in his throat had nothing to do with smoke inhalation.

"They have Arden."

The third time she got Smith's voice mail, Arden didn't bother leaving a message. How needy was she?

Instead, she put down her cell phone and focused on driving Val's old Jeep. She tried not to feel disappointed about Smith's continued silence, but, since her alternative was to worry about Jeff, her mind kept wandering back. Just because Smith wasn't returning her calls, even in an emergency, didn't mean he'd abandoned her.

Again.

After...

No. She knew such worries were an overreaction. So…why couldn't she shake her unease?

Likely he was involved in some kind of supersecret save-the-Comitatus mission for Greta. Surely he would call her as soon as he could. He wouldn't make love to her the way he had last night, wouldn't kiss her the way he had this morning, and then just…*leave.*

Some men, perhaps.

Not Smith.

Even if, living off the grid as he did, he *could* leave far more easily than most.

She didn't have her remote control for the outside gates—that was still in her own car, at her condominium near the light-rail station. But of course she knew the security code by heart. She breathed a sigh of relief as her family's gates slid closed behind her—Smith might be overprotective, but she *had* promised to be careful. She pulled to a stop just outside the four-car garage, surprised by the number of cars. Perhaps when Jeff refused to see a doctor, Daddy had brought the doctor to Jeff.

Leaving Val's Jeep in the driveway, Arden hurried through the side entrance—only to find the kitchen unusually still and empty. "Esperanza?"

She got no answer. Odd.

This wasn't Esperanza's day off.

"Jeff!" she called. "Dadd—" But a large, male palm suddenly pressed over her mouth.

Arden's cry of surprise didn't make it past the fleshy gag. Her attacker's forearm caught her, hard, across her throat, cutting off more breath.

Caught! Right there in the safety of her family kitchen.

She turned her head into the crook of her captor's elbow without even thinking—thank goodness for the bits of self-defense Smith had taught her, months ago. There, she could almost inhale past his soft, smothering fingers and the rich scent of Armani Black.

Prescott Lowell.

In her family's home!

Jeff, she thought, panicked even more for her loved ones than herself. *Daddy!*

If anything had happened to them because of her, because she'd drawn this secret-society melodrama to their front door, she would never forgive herself!

"It's no use struggling—" Lowell began.

He didn't finish. Finding her captor's foot with her own, Arden stomped with all her weight, scraping her heel down his shin before cracking down on his toes. At the same time, she clawed at the hand blocking her mouth and nose, finding and yanking viciously on the man's pinky finger.

She couldn't hear the snap over his howl of pain, over a surreal bit of music from the floor, but she felt it.

Gulping fresh air, Arden drove her elbow toward his throat—

He shoved her, hard, against the kitchen island before her blow connected. The marble countertop knocked precious breath from her. Somehow, through that, she recognized the ringtone on her phone. *Smith.*

Memory of Smith gave her the strength to kick out at the blur of movement that came at her.

Lowell's hands caught one of her ankles before she did damage. With a yank, he pulled her back from her brace on the countertop and into nothingness. Her jaw clipped marble as she fell to the tile floor, twisting a wrist. She rolled, catching the barest glimpse of Lowell and his fury. His face red, his eyes near white, he stomped viciously downward toward her face—

And, strangely, flew forward, right over her, into the glass-fronted cabinets.

Then—oh, thank heavens—Arden's daddy was there, big

and strong and perfectly safe. He stepped over her, loomed over her attacker.

"You dishonorable son of a whore!"

Lowell crabbed backward, sliding across the cabinet fronts, trapped. "She fought back!"

"Of course she fought back—she's a Leigh!" Her father hauled Arden's attacker up with one hand, backhanded him right back down with the other. "She's also of the blood! No common threat, to be *kicked*—" He kicked Lowell, hard, in the gut "—or *beaten* or even *shot.* Are we civilized—" another kick "—or are we not?"

Pulling herself to a kneeling position, Arden first blamed her confusion on the throbbing in her head. Nothing her father said made any sense!

Or—

No. She couldn't *let* it make sense.

"Don!" Another man appeared to pull her father off of her attacker, taking an offhand blow for his troubles. "Donaldson—listen to yourself!"

Her father stopped, panting. His wild eyes went from Lowell, still lying by the cabinets, to Arden, still kneeling beside the kitchen island. She realized that her phone had stopped ringing.

"Blood lets blood," he rasped, sounding oddly defeated for someone who'd just saved her and beaten down her attacker.

"Yes," agreed his companion. "But doesn't that count for Lowell blood, too? We'll have to justify our actions with his father, as well as with Stuart. Stop being so…Irish."

The way he forced a crooked smile at that, through the weight in the room—the way his eyebrows tilted in his effort to communicate—helped Arden place his identity even through her growing horror. Will Donnell.

Smith's father. Comitatus.

That frightened her in a way that made her want to shut her

yes, shake her head—stop time. She tried to pull herself up, and then her father was there, like the southern gentleman he was, assisting her to her feet. When she threw herself into his familiar arms, he stiffened.

So did she. Too much evidence. Too much proof. *No!*

Lowell protested. "I haven't betrayed anybody! She did."

"It's not betrayal if she doesn't know better!" Her father shot back over her head, his arms closing around her at last. See? Her suspicions were wrong. They had to be….

"We need to call the police," Arden managed, her voice raspy from the pressure Lowell had forced against it. Her mouth felt swollen where he'd tried to gag her. Her head, back and wrist throbbed from the marble island. "He broke in. He attacked me." But— "Where's Jeff? Daddy, where's Jeffie?"

"Hush, bunny. Jeff's at the Galleria."

So…he *wasn't* hurt? *No, no, no.* If Daddy had lied, that meant— "But his arm…"

"His arm is fine."

"It's your decision," said Donnell, quietly.

"She's got to be—" began Lowell, but now Donnell was the one who slapped him into silence.

"We *know!*" Smith's father agreed.

Finally, despite the pain, Arden stopped fighting the truth. Her father's call had been to lure her here. Lowell couldn't have infiltrated the Leigh estate without any of Daddy's top security catching him. Someone had sent the housekeeper away.

And then there were the words—*of the blood. Doesn't know any better.*

The dying sensation deep in her gut told her that she *did* understand, even if she didn't want to; should have understood long ago. Would have, if her family didn't matter so much. Her family had been everything. Maybe part of her *would* rather die than understand. But the rest of her…

Jeff was safe—for now. Smith loved her. The girls in Oak Cliff needed her.

Southern women had strength. Grit. So she faced the truth and the cold that swept through her like death.

Her father was also Comitatus. He'd hidden that from her. *Smith* had hidden that from her. Her life had always been made of lies.

"I'm okay, Daddy." Her soft words rang in her ears like someone else's, like she was hearing them from a television or radio. Patting his shoulder, she stepped back.

He let her, refused to meet her gaze.

"But we need to do something about this intruder," she insisted, as if she hadn't figured any of it out yet.

And when her father and Mr. Donnell glanced back to the panting, bloody excuse for a human still on the floor?

Arden dove for the exit. It took all her good sense not to detour for her purse—the need to call Smith felt that strong. She yanked the door inward, veered around it—

Too slow. Hands caught her back, horribly familiar hands. "Stop it," her father commanded as he'd once chided her about fidgeting in church or crying over a lost pageant. She struggled against his grip, but not hard enough. Even now, she couldn't summon up the desperation to stomp his foot or gouge at his eyes or try any other violent self-defense techniques.

Instinct had deserted her, because after nearly a quarter century of training, her instinct still said to trust her father. So he was Comitatus? So was Smith. That didn't make them bad, just...

Liars. All of them, liars.

"Arden, stop it!" her father demanded.

So she obeyed, defeated in far more ways than one.

* * *

All Smith wanted in the world was to get to Arden.

But when Greta stepped in his path before he could reach the door, he recognized the velvet-wrapped bundle in her hands by more than sight. He *felt* it.

He immediately knew, with the instincts of his fathers' fathers' fathers, that he *needed* it.

So why did he stop and wait for this, her third offer?

"Will you take the Sword of Aeneas with you?" asked the old woman, daughter of an exiled Comitatus member, descendent of heroes.

Smith swallowed around the oddest sense of destiny. "Yes."

What it lacked in poetry, it made up for in efficiency. And as she handed the antique to him, its weight in his hand, even through the velvet, felt—

Complete.

Smith reached under the wrapping, his palm drawn to the sword's grip as if through years of practice. At long last, he curled his fingers firmly around the grip.

And some power, some energy—*glimpses of firelight and molten metal, the shock of hammer on anvil, the absolute focus of duty*—curled around him.

"Trace will watch after you until we get back," he promised, hurrying out the front door as Mitch started his old car. For once, Trace didn't argue with him.

"Val's coming along," Mitch explained quickly out the window as Smith strode around to the passenger side. "Because Arden took her car, and because I'm too scared to tell her— *Holy crap!*" That last because Smith had let the velvet fall away from the sword as he took his place riding shotgun. "Okay, now I'm scared of you, too."

"Just drive," warned Smith, ignoring Mitch's double take and Val's doubtful grunt from the backseat.

Mitch drove.

"Guns are more practical," noted Val, supremely unimpressed.

Smith felt somehow blasphemous as he said, "What exactly makes you think I don't have my gun?"

But seriously. She was right.

Wasn't she?

When the old guesthouse was converted to her father's detached study, its walk-in closet became a storage and file room. That's where Arden found herself stowed, hands and feet tied, guarded by a particularly unlikely armed Comitatus member. Armed with a knife, that was.

What was it with these guys and knives?

Meanwhile her father, Smith's father and at least five other men had gathered in the larger room beyond to decide her fate.

At least, that's what she'd first thought they were talking about. But she overheard enough through the thin walls to realize that, in fact, they were meeting about Molly Johannes.

She felt oddly insulted. Heaven forbid the secret society let something as minor as the capture of a prodigal daughter get in the way of their he-man-woman-hater schemes!

It sounded as bad as Sibyl had predicted—a total smear campaign aimed to undermine the public's faith in female politicians. Ugly enough that she realized she had no desire to hear more—especially not her once-beloved father's role in all this. Instead, she tried to engage her guard in conversation. "You didn't gag me."

"You aren't making a lot of noise," responded Quinn Peters, pacing as best he could in the confined space. Arden had wondered what had happened to the fourth member of Smith's security company once Mitch and Trace showed up, but no time had seemed appropriate for asking.

Now she had her answer. Quinn hadn't left the Comitatus.

"What if I do make noise?"

He glanced toward her, a sad smile twisting his angular, strained face. Quinn always had seemed overly bookish and solemn, as if he should be wearing horn-rimmed glasses and a pocket protector…not that anybody in his social class would resort to either. Now he seemed bookish, solemn and conflicted.

"You won't," he assured her softly. "You've far too much dignity. Look at you." He gestured with his toothy knife. "You've got more di   tting there, tied and waiting your execution, than any one of   inner circle beyond that door."

"Then why are you on their side instead of mine?"

He paused in his pacing. "Do you know, you're the first person to ask me that?"

Arden waited, trying to be the picture of dignity he apparently saw.

Realizing that she expected an answer, Quinn shrugged one slim shoulder and started pacing again. "Let's just say I have student loans."

Arden sincerely hoped that wasn't his whole story. More important, though… "Daddy won't *execute* me."

"I wouldn't bet on that."

"Obviously," noted Arden, "I would."

"Don't underestimate our ability to compartmentalize. He lured you here in the first place, didn't he? You'd be smarter to club me over the head and take off out that attic crawl space up there. Speaking of which…" Leaning momentarily against the door to listen, Quinn frowned in concentration. "That's my cue. Promise me something?"

"You're hardly in a position to be asking favors!"

"Exactly. I didn't help you. I mean, neither did I abuse you like Lowell might have, what with him being psychotic. But I didn't help. This—" To her amazement, he tossed something toward her, something small and hard and heavy that she fumbled with her tied hands, dropped, then retrieved,

"—didn't come from me. Swear you won't tell *anyone.* Please."

It was a Swiss Army knife.

"Why didn't you give this to me sooner?" she demanded, opening it to start slicing at the ties across her ankles, but he cleared his throat and shook his head.

For a moment, he looked terrified.

Arden, the hostage, felt like the calm, controlled one here. But she hid the knife, and just in time.

The door cracked open, and Will Donnell leaned in. "Stuart's leaving."

Arden gave Smith's father her best shame-on-you glare. Damn right, she was dignified. But she could see he was doing a visual check on her ties, and in her head thanked Quinn for his quiet warning.

"Look, Mr. Donnell." Quinn glanced from the apparent elder to Arden and back. "I used to know Arden Leigh. We had mutual friends. She's a sweet lady. I'm sure if the elders reason with her—"

"Stuart," repeated Smith's father, "*is leaving.*"

Quinn shrugged. "And I'm with Stuart. Arden?" Then, apparently at a loss for the proper sentiment to give someone facing execution at the hands of his own society—Good luck? Have a nice day?—he just shrugged and escaped.

"It won't be long now," Donnell assured her with the same kind of false courtesy her father had shown her as they tied her hands and feet. Then he shut the door again, leaving her alone.

Arden started sawing at the ties with everything she had. The attic crawl space, Quinn had said. Beyond that would likely be a large vent, and freedom.

Freedom to do what? Reality as she'd known it remained in shambles.

But she could worry about that once she was safe.

Once she'd gotten back to Smith.

Free! Closing the knife and tucking it into her bra, Arden used the closet shelves to climb to the attic trapdoor and pushed it upward. Thank goodness she'd borrowed a pair of Val's slacks—cuffed and belted—and one of Val's plain T-shirts. The heels from yesterday's sundress ensemble were bad enough. She'd never been in a crawl space before, and would hate to do it in a skirt, especially with all the loose, cottony insulation.

She tried not to breathe deeply, but beggars couldn't be choosers.

An attachment on the knife came in handy to unscrew the bolts on the triangular gable vent—she owed Quinn Peters one hell of a thank-you basket, if she could send it anonymously. She had to stand on a storage box and broke a nail, but otherwise managed to lift the awkward metal plate into the attic with her, then to peek out across the manicured, afternoon yard that had been her lifelong home.

Her sanctuary.

Her base. Even now, just from habit, it felt safe. But she knew better.

Appearances could most certainly be deceiving.

Last time they'd met, the Comitatus had posted a guard. She'd figured out enough to realize that Lowell's job had been just that the first time he'd pulled a knife on her.

This time, she saw nobody. Just the security gates closing behind, she assumed, the departure of Quinn and this "Stuart" person. Hadn't Sibyl said something about Stuarts being bigwigs in the society?

Forcing herself to act without guarantees, she boosted herself up and out of the opening, turning midway to go feet first, then dropped awkwardly to the ground. She turned her ankle as she landed, but that wasn't enough to stop her.

Crouching low, Arden circled the old guest house that now served as her father's office—and nearly tripped over the unconscious guard. *What…?*

"Arden!" Male arms closed around her from the side, not in attack but in relief. But Arden didn't feel at all relieved as she returned the enthusiastic hug.

The last person she'd wanted to find here was her baby brother, Jeff.

Chapter 14

This wasn't at all what Jeff had expected.

When the older guys at camp whispered rumors about initiation, powerful connections, inner circles, he'd loved the idea. An ancient secret society of heroes? He'd always suspected they were special. How cool was it that they really *were?*

He couldn't wait to turn fifteen and join, too.

The only reason he hadn't mentioned anything to his dad was, he didn't want to narc on his secret-spilling friends. He didn't want anyone thinking he couldn't keep secrets, either. So when a couple of Dad's most important colleagues from out of town had arrived to stay over last night, and more big names from the best Dallas/Fort Worth families showed up today, Jeff pretended not to know that something wonderfully huge must be going down.

Secret-societywise, that is.

He hadn't offered to leave for the day—just in case they

meant to initiate him early, which would completely rock. But when Dad made noises about his plans for the afternoon, Jeff invented some. He even had Esperanza drop him off at the Galleria before she headed out for her unexpected day off.

But then he caught a cab right back. Back to their Highland Park neighborhood, that is. He was smarter than to show up right in front of the house.

See? He could be secretive, too. And seriously. What almost-fifteen-year-old couldn't sneak around his own house without getting caught?

Then Jeff's day took a terrible turn. His sister, Arden, had always said eavesdroppers seldom heard good of themselves. But Jeff had thought he'd hear good of *someone*. Instead, listening at the window, he heard Dad playing a recording of Arden's voice. "Who else is in this secret society of yours? Why are they interested in me or the state comptroller?"

Cool, thought Jeff. He didn't know exactly what a state comptroller did, but it sounded important. He also felt kind of proud of Arden for figuring whatever it was out.

Sure, women weren't supposed to know about the society. But seriously. Arden rocked.

Then Mr. Donnell said, "You don't have to do this."

Jeff shook off a shiver of unease and wondered, *Do what?*

Whatever it was, Dad didn't sound happy. "You're one to talk. This is your traitor's fault."

"He left my protection when he left the brotherhood," said Mr. Donnell, which made Jeff wonder if they were talking about his son, Arden's boyfriend, Smith. But why would Smith leave the brotherhood?

Jeff didn't hate Smith. Other than that whole kissing-Arden business. Arden seemed okay with it, and Smith had been cool to teach him how to fence.

Dad said that Arden had left his protection when she left home. "Now she's endangering us. It must be stopped." *Stopped?*

Jeff didn't like the sound of that at all. He seriously disliked hearing his own father lie to leave a message telling Arden that he—Jeff—had hurt himself. Dad was using *Jeff* to get to *Arden?* That didn't sound real heroic.

Jeff knew Arden would come right away. She loved him. Jeff loved her. Their dad loved both of them…didn't he?

But over the next hour, Jeff learned that, no. Apparently Dad didn't.

He also learned that he—Jeff—wasn't a hero at all. He was just a stupid, scared kid. Stupid, because he kept thinking that if he just watched long enough, instead of interfering, his worst fears would be disproved. The society would turn out to have such noble goals that everything would explain itself. That's why he didn't call Arden back and tell her not to come. That's why he didn't warn her away when she arrived. He had to be mistaken, right? Their dad would only give her a stern talking-to, not anything worse.

Right?

Scared, because nobody could be that stupid. And once he knew that for sure—once Dad and Mr. Donnell and that other guy dragged Arden from the kitchen entrance and across the lawn to Dad's office—he had no excuse but fear. Arden's hair had fallen loose, all messy like from when she used to wrestle him into submission so he'd let her kiss on him… He'd always let her win, but still. Her shirt had pulled half out of her oversized pants, and Arden never let her clothes get messy. Blood darkened her swelling lip. She'd looked dazed.

They were holding Arden prisoner.

Jeff's Arden. Arden, who'd always taken care of him. Arden, who'd tutored him in history and English lit, and taught him how to waltz for his first academy dance. Arden, who'd held him in the night for weeks, right after Mom died, and yet let him pretend he hadn't been crying when day came again.

No matter what Dad's reason, or whatever stupid secrets she might have learned, Jeff knew soul-deep that treating his sister like that just wasn't right. And he had no idea what to do about it.

The secret-society guys outnumbered him. He supposed he could try calling the cops, but his friend at camp, Connor, had bragged that the society ran the police. *Smith,* Jeff thought then. Smith Donnell cared about Arden, and he apparently wasn't with the society anymore. Smith could help.

But Jeff didn't know Smith's number. And he feared that if he used his cell phone to call 411, much less the Donnell residence in Fort Worth, someone would somehow track it, and they'd know he was here, and then nobody would ever help Arden. So he didn't do anything. Just hid.

Like a big, scared baby. Except…

Scared or not, Jeff needed to save Arden. He didn't have a knife of his own—not like the cool, toothy weapons the older guys at camp had—and the idea of using a kitchen knife on anyone made him queasy. So he got his dad's titanium driver out of his golf bag and took it with him. Just in case.

Hiding in the bushes outside his father's office, Jeff had a chance to watch the blond guard they'd left patrolling the area. *Just one.* The door to the office opened and three men left, a redheaded man in the lead, with two others following him. Jeff stayed down—but noticed how the guard stopped to watch the trio drive away.

Three less, Jeff thought hopefully. But from the sound of things inside, at least a half-dozen men remained.

Then he heard a faint noise above him, coming from a triangular air vent under the eaves.

An air vent? What would anyone be doing with—

But Jeff excelled at sneaking…and maybe at wishful thinking. He thought maybe, just maybe, he knew why someone would fiddle with the vent cover from inside.

Hearing the big blond guard coming, Jeff circled the other direction to get behind him. God, the man seemed tall.

Jeff tightened his hands around the grip of the driver. He took one careful step, then another, closer and closer.

And then—

Well, then he walloped the guard from behind, right in the head, with the golf club. The guy didn't fall down right away. He stumbled sideways and tried to look over his shoulder at Jeff, and Jeff readied to swing again, thinking, *oh God, oh God...*

But then the man fell. Funny. Like he'd lost his balance.

Jeff stared down at him, so scared he could have thrown up. The club fell from his numb fingers. Had he killed him? Had someone heard? What would he do when they came to check?

But then he saw—

"Arden!"

No, no, no, no, no. Her one solace had been that nobody else whom she loved had been in danger. Now...

"What are you *doing* here?" she demanded, even as she began to drag Jeff across the backyard, toward the house and the phone. "Daddy said you were—"

"—at the mall. I lied. Arden, I'm sorry..." He gasped between words, fighting tears he clearly believed himself too old to shed.

Such a big, brave fourteen.

"It doesn't matter," she assured him, and it didn't. "What's important is that we *go!*"

But it was already too late.

"And where would you go, bunny?" called her father with his old presence, crossing the yard toward them. Five other men, Will Donnell and a bruised Prescott Lowell among them, fanned out.

Jeff's heavy inhalation sounded snuffly to Arden's protective ear, but he squared his shoulders and stepped between her and their approaching father. He was holding, she realized, a golf club. Like a sword. "You go, Arden. I'll hold them off."

"Not without you." She tugged on his arm. "Come on!"

"I'm your brother. It's my job to protect you."

"Protect me by running!" Too late. The circle of Comitatus had closed behind her.

"Don't touch her!" Jeff's voice cracked as he cut the air in front of him with the club, holding the other men at bay.

Their father stopped, just out of reach. "Son, you don't understand."

"I understand you lied. I understand you let them *tie her up!*"

"But you don't know why, or what she's threatening."

"Arden would never threaten anyone!" Again, Jeff swung the club, almost throwing himself off balance in the effort. He didn't remember Smith's lesson, Arden thought with a sad, surreal sense of distraction. It wouldn't do any good.

Especially not with several of the other suited Comitatus leaders drawing long, toothy knives from beneath their tailored suit jackets.

"You're wrong, boy. She threatens all of us, *especially* you. She threatens your very future. Perhaps she didn't do it on purpose, but that doesn't make her any less dangerous."

"I don't care!"

But he didn't see the pair of men—including Prescott Lowell—creeping up behind him. Arden stepped up against his back, fumbling open her too-small jackknife, facing this newest threat for him. Lowell remained unarmed, for once. Somehow, that didn't seem to make him any less dangerous.

"But you will," their father continued in that soothing, sensible tone that had always meant security and wisdom. "Someday you will. Don't throw everything away for fleeting sentimentality, boy."

In this, at least, she still agreed with her father. She couldn't let Jeff suffer—and what she saw in Lowell's eyes, as his met hers, was a hunger to inflict pain. "Will you keep him safe if I come willingly?" she asked.

Jeff flinched against her shoulder blades. "Arden, no!"

"Of course I will," said her father.

"Swear. On everything you hold sacred, you swear that Jeff will be okay."

"I swear."

She stared at Lowell's silent fury and knew this was the best she could manage. Besides, Jeff already knew too much. They might as well see this to the end.

Either her father really was capable of deliberately hurting her, perhaps even killing her, or he wasn't.

Either way, there was only one way for her and Jeff to find out.

"Then I surrender," she agreed, with all the grace she had in her. "To you, Daddy. Not—" she pointed at Lowell "—to this one."

"Arden, no!" wailed Jeff—but he was too late. In seconds he'd been disarmed and was being steered as gently as possible, considering his struggle, toward their father's study. Daddy followed, holding her by one wrist, as if she might still make a dash for it—without Jeff? He should know her better than that. Then again, how well had she known him?

Prescott Lowell sidled uncomfortably close, "Stupid." He teased. "Your brother would have been safe either way. He's your father's heir. He's of the blood. Why do you suppose your boyfriend is still walking arou—"

"You might learn," her father warned, "that even those of the blood can go too far, boyo."

Lowell's grin did nothing to cover his hatred toward Arden or her father, but despite all the secrets he'd kept, despite his betrayal of her, Arden knew one thing about her father. She knew that tone of voice.

No matter what happened to her, Prescott Lowell wasn't going to get much better.

She was too much of a lady—or a pragmatist—to find that especially comforting.

Fouling up security systems was a lot easier when one had installed them. Smith and Mitch used everything in their arsenal, from hacking into the system with a WiFi laptop to physically shimmying up a telephone pole to jamb the pivot function on an outdoor surveillance camera. The former bought them time. The latter bought them a temporary blind spot from which to approach the backyard.

They knew not to go in the front door. There was honor…and then there was a real chance to find and rescue Arden.

Easy choice.

Mitch closed the laptop and slid it back into his satchel. "If she's here, they don't have any security feeds on her."

"She's in the study," said Smith, peering over the yard's wall and past the wishing well, past the trees. He couldn't say how he knew that for sure. The study shades were down, but that wasn't uncommon in August. Still, he could sense it, as surely as if Arden was calling to him.

To him, or to the Sword of Aeneas.

"We just have to take out that guard without him sounding an alarm."

Smith knew the sentry this time—a guy named Charlie Morris, from the area, two years older than him. Had they learned their lesson about newcomers from Lowell?

Shame. Smith would have loved a chance to hurt Lowell, and he didn't want to hurt someone he knew. Morris could have been Smith or Mitch, barely a year ago. He might not know just how corrupt a society he'd joined.

So many of them didn't know.

No throat-slitting on this one.

"I'll create the distraction," announced Val, clambering over the fence. "You two make the best of it."

"I don't know, that might not—" But Smith found himself addressing air. "Dammit!"

Val loped across the yard, crouching behind the wishing well just before Morris came into sight again—stupid Morris, not varying his pattern. She used the cover of the stone well to strip off her shirt, leaving only a stretched white tank top, and shimmy awkwardly out of her jeans, revealing a pair of red boxers. Pulling the tie from her hair, she shook out its thick, kinky darkness. Checking to make sure that the guard had continued around the study, she sauntered toward the building more slowly, like a wrong-side-of-town vixen who didn't mean any real trouble.

Who just happened to be hiding a Saturday Night Special behind her back.

"Holy mother of wow," whispered Mitch.

Smith only knew he had to get to the building before Val's confrontation lost its element of surprise. Neither the climbing nor the running got easier holding an antique sword…and yet he wouldn't have put it down for anything.

"—the side gate, over there," the woman was explaining as Smith, still catching his breath from the race across the backyard, crept up behind Morris. On the downside, Val Diaz had none of the flirty tics that really made for a great distraction—no hip swaying, no giggly smiles. On the upside, she did a damned good job not letting her gaze track him as he moved into her line of sight. "You mean, you've never gone pool hopping in the fancy neighborhoods before?"

An honorable man would tap Morris's shoulder, let him face his attacker.

Smith guessed, as he slowly and silently stood, that he was done with honor.

"Look, miss, this is private property—" A light tap on the back of his head from the sword's pommel silenced Morris. He fell like a brick at Smith's feet.

"Look!" Mitch carried Val's discarded clothes when he caught up. Without a thank-you, she cinched Morris's hands and feet with plastic riot cuffs and tucked her shirt into his mouth as a makeshift gag. "Someone moved the vent to the attic. Do you think it's a trap?"

"Let me stand on your shoulders and I'll find out," offered Val.

Mitch hurried to do just that. In the meantime, Smith crept close enough to the office to overhear snatches of conversation beyond a closed, shaded window. He caught phrases like "the necessity of secrecy," and "she had her chance," and "the only honorable solution."

A voice he clearly recognized as Arden's. "If this is what you consider honor, no wonder your society's rotting from the inside."

Everything in him went still. *They really had Arden.*

"We're clear," Mitch hissed down to him. "Come on up, and we can get the footage we—"

"Start filming without me." Setting his shoulders, Smith looked at the door—then looked down at the double-edged, flared sword in his hand. The jeweled hilt. The warm tint to the blade.

The Sword of Aeneas, huh?

On the one hand, it would really get in the way as he shot any Comitatus bastards who weren't in a mood to negotiate.

On the other hand, there could be as many as six or seven men in there. His revolver only held six bullets. Unless he could convince the Comitatus to stand in a nice line, he could use a secondary, backup weapon.

His sword would, at the very least, put their ceremonial knives to shame.

"You're kidding, right, Smith?" But Mitch vanished into the attic after Val. He knew Smith well enough by now.

Carefully, deliberately, Smith turned the knob on the door into Leigh's guest-house study. In slow increments, he edged it inward just enough to keep it unlatched—drama could always use a little assist, when possible.

"—leaving it up to Leigh," announced a voice that made Smith's stomach clench in a completely different way.

Dad.

Then, as Smith shifted the sword to his off hand and drew his revolver from his SOB holster, Donaldson Leigh made a decision. "This is centuries of tradition, an ancient covenant. It's bigger than any of us. I'm sorry, bunny. Truly…"

"No!" wailed a voice that sounded way too young for any Comitatus—

And Smith kicked the office door in. Hard. Loud. Satisfying.

Thanks to the element of surprise, as well as his drawn gun, Smith got a minute to appreciate the tableau before him. His own father, Will Donnell, stood to the side, holding a worse-for-wear Prescott Lowell by the arm. Three other Comitatus members, familiar from Smith's own days in the society, joined those two in their surprised stillness. In the center of the room, Donaldson Leigh seemed to be facing off against a remarkably composed Arden. Her less composed younger brother tried futilely to stay between them.

Arden…

Her beautiful eyes flared in surprise. Recognition lit her heart-shaped face, pulled at her full lips—only to draw into a fiercer scowl.

Apparently he'd ticked her off again somehow.

By now, Smith was more than used to that.

"Sorry, fellas," he announced, smiling widely at his audience to keep from growling at them when he recognized the swelling of Arden's lip, the bruising shadowing her jaw. "I forgot the secret knock.

"Did I miss anything?"

One moment, Arden had been listening to her father choose his secret society over her. Worse? He apparently meant to kill her to do it.

Part of her refused to believe it, but she could no longer trust that part of her. Only her experience in pageants and poise— that, and a need to keep Jeff calm, to think as clearly as possible—had kept her from screaming and clawing at him.

The next moment, the door had exploded open and Smith, *her* Smith, stood backlit by August sunshine, an incongruously decorative sword in one hand and a revolver in the other. Never had the bandages on his arms looked more like gauntlets.

Smith had come for her. He was her hero, after all.

Then Arden recognized the extreme danger that put him in. If her own father would willingly kill her, then Smith…

The *idiot!* He'd come for *her?* Did he think she couldn't handle matters herself?

Other than this surrounded-by-enemies, slated-for-execution business.

"I forgot the secret knock," Smith faux-apologized, cockier than ever. She wondered if he'd practiced that line. "Did I miss anything?"

"You missed the part where you were banished from this society," snarled her father.

"Yeah. About that. I've decided I don't accept banishment. Now step away from Arden and Jeff."

"Don't *accept?*" parroted Lowell.

"Smith…" Mr. Donnell shook his head. "Don't make this any worse."

"Any worse than what, Dad? Whatever could you pillars of society have been planning?" Smith's mocking expression hardened. "If Arden and Jeff leave with me, we don't have a problem."

"You know that can't happen." Her father, again. "She knows too much—and I blame you. Her blood will be on your hands as much as on mine."

Jeff tried to push Arden farther back with his body. Keeping her hands on his lanky shoulders, to brace him as much as herself, Arden refused to move, even to shake off her father's grip. Not until the path to the door cleared.

She'd given herself up once already, to protect Jeff. She wouldn't endanger him in a premature dash for minimal safety.

Smith's father said, "You spent almost ten years in the society, boy. You understand the obligation we have to protect our secrecy, our preeminence."

Smith rolled his eyes. "Did nobody actually pay attention to *why* I left?"

"You left," dared Lowell, "because you couldn't cut it."

Arden almost rolled her own eyes at the ridiculousness of his claim, until she saw Smith's stubborn chin come up. Surely he wouldn't let Lowell *provoke* him into a fight, would he?

Then again…

"I *could* cut it," Smith insisted. "I just chose *not* to cut it. Not in some corrupt farce of what we were once supposed to be."

"Bullshit." And Lowell wrenched away from Mr. Donnell, his body language radiating challenge. "You never gave a damn about the Comitatus."

"The Comitatus gave me something to believe in!" The words that ripped from Smith tore at Arden's heart, too. At last, he'd admitted it. And not just that he had really belonged.

Why he'd belonged.

"It gave me a direction," he echoed. "And all the petty,

power-hungry *bullying* that they've taken on as a new mission statement took that away from me. If this is all that's left of a great society, then we need to take it out back and shoot it. *Let Arden go.*"

In answer, her father's grip on her arm only tightened. He wasn't trying to hurt her. She suspected she could twist away from him if she had to. But that left several other Comitatus members to get through before she and Jeff reached the door.

She didn't like their odds of making it safely, especially after Lowell snatched a knife from the lax hand of one of the older men. She didn't like their odds of making it safely.

"You and firearms," Lowell taunted. "It was decided centuries ago—any commoner can use a gun. But you're too much of a coward to fight me like a gentleman."

"Arden's safety is worth more than elitist traditions," Smith insisted.

God, she loved him.

"Then give *her* the gun, and she'll be safe," suggested Lowell. He even clucked like a chicken, to complete his caricature. "Let's see if that shiny party favor of yours can stand up against a traditional blade. Or are you—"

Smith took two steps, and Arden found herself detached from her father and brother both, with the weight of a revolver in her hands. "Do whatever you have to," Smith murmured into her ear, holding his sword between them and danger. He smelled disturbingly like smoke.

Then he was gone from her, shifting the blade to his dominant hand in preparation. For a moment, he paused. Blinked slowly, as if distracted by something. Then he obviously shook it off, standing taller than ever.

The pistol grip in Arden's hands still radiated his heat.

"Challenge made," announced Smith, circling his opponent. "Challenge accepted. By society rules, nobody else can interfere. Oh, and by the way?"

Lowell, brandishing his toothy knife, waited.

Smith smirked. "Bite me."

Oh…*sugar.*

Chapter 15

Smith began the standard salute, touching the bejeweled hilt of the Aeneas sword to his heart, his lips—and the buzz that had filled his head, from the moment he'd shifted it to his dominant hand, amplified.

Time swallowed him.

He saw darkness. Mankind's near helplessness against animals' hunger—against one another's evil. And then—then, the innovations that changed the world.

Bronze.

Then iron.

Then steel.

And he knew. *He got it.* This wasn't just a sword of heroes. This blade, and the blades like it, and the men worthy enough to wield them, carried the hope of humanity.

If ever magic existed, if ever early man became god, he did so by transforming base elements through smoke, through heat, through sweat into instruments of pure grace. Everything became metaphor. Smelted ores—cleansed of impurity, fused together, no one of them strong enough on its own. Crucibles of molten metal cast, hardened into bars, then forged in coals. From earth to fire, glowing red, burning to orange, then searing into white. Hammered toward perfection, no gentle process, but beautiful in its violence, again, again. Folded. Reformed. Then—water. Quenched in a rush of steam, to harden it, to temper it. Tested and retested. Those blades which cracked, or warped or shattered on impact were discarded without sentimentality.

Everything went to the end result. Perfect weapons—hard, yet flexible. As beautiful as they were powerful, and, oh, the power. The person with the best sword won. Ruled. Passed on his blade as he passed on his legacy. Swordsmith—Hephaestus? Warrior—Achilles? Emperor—Aeneas?

Every one of them represented in the next, hero to hero, through the millennia.

By this sword.

Then—Smith was back, lifting the sword upward into the air, to finish the salute, and to finish its quest. It had been forged for one purpose, to be used toward the good of all.

And here he stood, ready to accept the responsibility of doing just that.

One freakin' fight at a time.

Lowell lunged mid-salute, full-body. Bastard.

This was why Smith had instructed Jeff to attack sword first…and he felt oddly as if the sword in his hand knew it. Pivoting onto one leg, he stopped Lowell with a boot in his gut. He bent his own knee to ease the weight of the younger man's momentum. He blocked the knife with the Aeneas sword—knew it wouldn't shatter, however old it really was—and kicked Lowell backward. Hard.

"You need a bigger sword."

Stumbling, Lowell regained his balance against a dark-paneled bookcase. "Tradition's good enough for me."

"Swords *are* traditional, dumbass." Smith smacked Lowell's knife hand with the flat of his blade. Then, following the movement full circle, he flicked the knife free with the full weight of his sword.

All that was left was to kick the knife under a chair, as soon as it hit the floor, and level the Aeneas sword at Lowell's throat.

That easy. On a gut level, Smith knew part of that was the Sword of Aeneas. But only because of what it stirred deep within him.

He raised his empty hand high, like a calf-roper in the rodeo signaling time to stop the clock. Lowell glared—but reluctantly held up both his hands in brooding surrender.

"You defended with your body," noted Jeff, who'd maybe paid attention to the other day's lesson after all. "Cool!"

Smith knew better than to preen, with Arden still in danger. "Well, that was fun. Now if you guys are finished with the younger Leighs—"

"We are not." *Hell.* Arden's father remained as big and determined as ever.

"Daaad!" wailed Jeff. Smith remembered the first time he'd realized his father wasn't as honorable as he'd imagined. It wasn't that long ago. "He *won!*"

"He won against Lowell." Over by the bookcase, Lowell's mouth fell open in silent protest, but Leigh faced the other men with natural presence, natural leadership. A surface semblance of leadership, anyway. "Smith himself admitted that their weapons were mismatched. More important, nobody among us named Lowell as our champion—nor would we be so foolish as to do so. If a duel were to be official, it must follow tradition."

"There was already a duel!" protested Arden, the revolver hanging at her side.

Smith widened his eyes at her, jerked his chin toward the gun.

She raised it again. She and Jeff had backed into a corner, more than an arm's reach from any of the Comitatus. Of that, at least, he approved.

"That was a rout," her father snapped back, as if winning were a character flaw.

"It's okay," Smith assured her. "That was just practice? Fine. Let's establish some legitimate conditions and duel for real."

"If you lose, you leave here. Alone. And you never, *never* come back." Worse? That demand came from Smith's own father.

Smith ignored his gaze. *Leave and never come back?* He'd heard that before.

"Not just that." Donaldson Leigh moved books from one of his built-in shelves, dropping them loudly to the marble floor. "You will have a half-hour head start. If any Comitatus member sees you again—" *thud* "—they will be under orders to kill you. We tried to be lenient with your exile, because you're of the blood, but—" *crash* "—no more. You have flaunted our indulgence and, worse—" With a final sweep of books, he turned with a long wooden box in his hands and laid it on his desk. "You destroyed my daughter."

"You're being ridiculous," protested Arden, her full lips parted, her beautiful eyes flashing. "He did no such thing!"

Leigh wouldn't even look at her.

"I was researching the Comitatus before Smith ever came back!"

Again, she got no reaction.

"Daddy…" she whispered. Then she narrowed her eyes, lifted her stubborn little chin—and was done with him. Smith had seen that dark expression before. Now, though, he saw the extent of the pain that had prompted it.

For that alone, he hoped he got to fight Leigh—and kick his butt. "And what about Arden, if I lose?"

"If you lose," Leigh clarified, opening the wooden box, "it will be no business of yours *what* happens to Arden."

"Oookay, then—"

"Smith!" protested Arden. He shrugged apologetically to-

ward her. It wasn't as if he had any option, besides the duel, tha
wouldn't end with her under Leigh's control. Well…nothin,
except killing him, which—no. Or sic'ing Mitch and Val on th
lot of them, but mentioning their presence would kind of blov
the secret-weapon part of their nearness. For now, Smith wa
happy with those two just capturing this meeting on tape.

He'd just have to win, was all.

He liked to think the blade agreed.

"Here are *my* conditions." He swung the Aeneas sword
trying to summon up some of his earlier cockiness. "When
win, you release all hold on Arden and Jeff, both."

"No." No bargaining. No nothing. Damn, Leigh was con
fident.

"Ard, could I have that gun back?"

"You cannot take Jeff," clarified Leigh, one hand in th
box. Briefly, Smith worried that he had a gun in there. But i
Leigh still believed even in twisted, Comitatus honor… "He':
my only son. My *heir.*"

Smith's dad winced. Unlike with Arden, Smith took a sel
fish pleasure in *his* distress.

"Then how's this? Jeff gets to choose whether or not to g
into the Comitatus, with no undue pressure—no threats o
violence, no financial manipulation, nothing. If you try to forc
him in any way, you're undermining everything even you thin
the Comitatus stand for. But Arden gets a free pass. She keep
her trust fund. She is never under threat from your society again."

Leigh glowered at his daughter—who, holding Smith'
revolver in both hands, glowered right back. God, she was mag
nificent. Finally he said, "If she promises to keep our secret."

"Like she was such a big threat before," scoffed Smith.

Then Arden disproved him. "That depends on whether yo
drop your plans to ruin Molly Johannes." Oh, yeah. Her.

"Um…yeah," added Smith, embarrassed to have forgotten
"And you drop your plans against the state comptroller."

Her father's face flushed red, but Arden didn't back down. "You allowed me to host a fundraiser for her in this very house," she noted. "That means you offered her hospitality. In what society has it ever been honorable to turn on your own guests?"

"Damn few," Smith agreed.

"You've no say in our decisions," Leigh warned her. "If you want safety, you stay out of society business!"

He was lucky, thought Smith, that she didn't shoot him right there. Or Smith when he said, "She'll take it."

Arden glared. She couldn't know that they already had enough proof on tape to clear Molly's reputation when the time came.

He seriously hoped her attitude toward him improved when she found out.

"You didn't ask for your own safety," his father noted.

Smith laughed. "You're saying you'd give it to me?"

"Not in a million years." Leigh removed a sword from the wooden box—a beautiful saber with an ornate brass knuckle-guard and wired-leather grip. Smith could make out the letters CS engraved into the blade, amidst other flourishes. *Confederate States.*

He tightened his grip on the sword of Aeneas. "Last condition. Win or lose, you're to grant immunity to Greta Kaiser in Oak Cliff. Lowell here tried to burn her house down earlier today. She's fine," he added quickly, at Arden's gasp. "But that kind of harassment ends now. Either way, Greta Kaiser gets a free pass. Her house becomes sanctuary. No Comitatus presence within a five-block radius of it—which, incidentally, includes Arden's recreation center."

Leigh scoffed. Arden, though—Arden stared at Smith as if she understood. He might not be able to stay with her, no more than Aeneas had stayed with Dido. Death or further exile would probably see to that. But the least that he could do was secure her other love.

Donaldson said, "I don't—"

"Safe status in Oak Cliff," Smith insisted, "or I take tha gun from Arden and start shooting."

His father tried not to look startled. "Don't make threat you won't see through."

"I'm not honorable, remember? A blight on our family legacy, you said. Arden probably wouldn't forgive me, but a least she'd be alive."

Silence. Better than an instant no.

"Greta's an old blind woman," Smith insisted. "And she' *of the blood.* Don't any of you recognize the name Kaiser Time was that the society took care of widows and orphan of the blood."

Maybe Leigh liked that Smith had appealed to his honor Maybe he even had some remnants left. He nodded. "It's deal. Before all witnesses."

"Before all witnesses," echoed the other men in the room Jeff looked, wide-eyed, from one to another.

"You should hear yourselves," chided Arden. "You can' really mean to stake this much on some foolish sword fight!"

Leigh swung his blade, as if adjusting to the weight of it Good. Just the opponent Smith wanted. "As the senior mem ber present, I name myself champion for this contest. Doe anyone here object?"

"*I* object!" insisted Arden. At the same time, Lowell said "You've got to be kidding! Why are you giving him any con cessions at all?"

"You—" Leigh pointed his sword at the younger man "—have shown no grasp of the responsibilities of our position You have no say in this."

Then he came around the desk and faced Smith.

"Stop it," repeated Arden, more quietly.

"Just a moment," said Smith to his opponent—and turned and stepped to Arden's side, and kissed her.

Thoroughly.

His free hand wove into her thick, black, Irish hair. His lips worshipped her. His soul…

Just in case. Sooner or later, after all, even heroes lost.

He took some small comfort in the fact that she kissed him back, far more passionately than her ladylike exterior would imply. He took even more comfort from the sense of rightness about this. Apparently he had more Comitatus left in him than he'd thought. Because the person he'd once been—the rebellious youth who'd found direction in the idea that the people with power could use it for good—now filled him with ideals he thought he'd lost with his credit rating and his trust fund. Lowell was right about one thing. Guns *were* inelegant, brutish, pragmatic.

If needed to save Arden, Smith could manage all three.

But as long as she had the ability to save herself…

Wrenching himself away from her and back to Leigh, Smith touched the hilt of his sword to his heart, his lips, then the sky. *That honor guide my heart. That my words guide my actions. That something greater guide my body.*

He felt strangely gratified when the older, stockier man did the same.

And then—

Then Leigh went on the offensive. Fast. Strong.

And expert.

Smith felt an honest grin stretch his own mouth. No, he didn't want Arden at risk. He didn't want Jeff trapped as he'd been trapped. He didn't want Greta harmed. And yet…

The same idealist he'd once been relished the skilled attacks that he and his blade blocked, parried, ducked.

This, at least, would be a fair fight.

Stupid, Arden kept thinking. *Stupid, stupid, stupid.* How…*male* of them, to think that they could resolve something as significant as Greta's safety—as her own life!—by fighting about it with antique swords.

She shifted the not-insignificant weight of Smith's revolver, which she held with both hands, slightly more to the left and reviewed everything she knew from summer camp about firing a gun. Revolvers had no safety—check. Situate her target, whatever—*whoever*—that was over the sight, like a lollipop onto a stick—check. And when the time came, squeeze instead of pull the trigger.

Neither her fate nor Jeff's would have a damned thing to do with this sword fight, even if she had to kill her own father to ensure it. She prayed it wouldn't come to that. But the man she'd met this afternoon apparently *wasn't* her father, not the way she'd thought she knew him.

The man she thought she knew had always taught her to fight back against people who threatened or bullied her.

Whatever you say, Daddy.

And yet…

Despite the men surrounding her who, excepting Smith and Jeff, apparently held her life in so little esteem. Despite her belief that this fight could prove nothing beyond who was better at swinging swords. Despite all that, something far more powerful seemed to be going on here.

It was kind of thrilling to watch.

How many twenty-first century women got to see their lover *duel* for them?

Arden had never studied fencing, but she quickly grasped the basics. There was no taking of turns, or all the dancing footwork and rapid exchange of blows she expected from the movies…these swords looked a lot heavier. Smith and her father circled each other, sometimes attacking with great swipes toward the other's head, sides or gut, sometimes putting all their strength into parrying those blows in ringing clashes of metal and strength. Her father had more breadth than Smith. His blows forced her lover to retreat, to pivot, to duck out of the way.

"Duels are rarely fights to the death," murmured Will Donnell. Arden couldn't tell if he was reassuring her or himself.

But of all the many things Arden had to worry about on this awful day, Smith losing the fight wasn't one of them. Because Smith *did* parry, and dodge and block every one of her father's attacks.

And unlike her father, Smith wasn't tiring.

Being Smith, he chose instead to play the smart-ass.

"Don't you think there's a *reason*—" he ducked a left-to-right swing of her father's sword with an upward thrust of his own, locking blade to blade. His arms shook as he heaved the older man back from him "—that the world moved beyond trial by combat?"

"No good one." Did her father show less grace as he swung the Leigh family saber downward, as if to cleave Smith's skull?

Smith stopped it with his own fascinating, ancient-looking blade, sinking at the knees to absorb the strike.

"Tradition is everything," her father panted—and stumbled back, but didn't fall, as Smith cast off both him and his sword. "Once, it was everything to you. What happened, boy?"

Smith, circling him warily, growled, "I found Arden."

She caught her breath. Did he really mean that?

"It was one thing when I was a teenager, to think that we knew better than anyone else. Anyone not lucky enough to be born wealthy, male…Comitatus, I mean. But then I met more of the rest of the world. Then I fell for your daughter."

"Shut up." Not the words of a Southern gentleman. Her father hadn't retreated—he only pivoted, slowly, to keep pace with Smith's slow perimeter. But he no longer stood in charge. Even Arden could see it.

When Smith attacked—"Sword first," Arden heard Jeff

whisper—it started a faster series of swings and parries, each move exaggerated by the weight and arc of the weapon.

Then Smith was circling again, his footwork as sure as a dancer's in his worn, off-brand athletic shoes.

A swordsman.

"You really think we're better than her? God knows people like Lowell aren't. Arden doesn't need either one of us to do her thinking for her," he continued—unexpected balm to her heart. "She can even do without our protection. The only dangers she's faced this week came from your damned traditions."

"She shouldn't have delved into—"

"Why the hell not?" Now Smith and her father just stood, swords ready but still, each catching his breath. "*We* wouldn't tell her anything, so why *shouldn't* she find the answers on her own? She's an adult. She's a free agent. And in case you haven't noticed, she's pretty damned smart."

Her father leveled his blade at Smith, more in warning than attack. "You have no business telling me about my own daughter."

Smith smacked the saber away from his face with a sharp ring of steel on steel. "I'm not the jerk who's considering doing God-knows what to her to protect his precious tradition!"

Both men stood, gazes locked, chests rising and falling over their swords.

We could make it to the door now, Arden thought, noting everyone's distraction—but no. This was far, *far* too important. She had the gun. She could protect Jeff…and, if necessary, Smith.

Smith shook his head. "The hell with all of you. Any tradition that would require a man to turn on the people he most cares about isn't a tradition worth preserving." He looked at the sword in his hand as if he meant to toss it onto the ground in pained defeat—not defeat at the hands of her father, but at the death of his ideals.

If so much hadn't been riding on this fight, Arden suspected he would do just that.

"To be a leader," chided her father, "one must be willing to sacrifice."

Smith barked out a harsh laugh. "When did it become honorable to sacrifice *what isn't yours* in the first place?"

Arden saw her father take three breaths, each deeper than the last, as if girding himself for something. When he lunged forward, he attacked more with his body than with his saber. It seemed an ungainly move, even to Arden's amateur eye.

In a fluid spin, Smith stepped into the attack, past the danger of his opponent's sword. He body-checked her father even as he grasped his sword arm with his free hand and, in one final clash of blades, disarmed him.

The Civil War saber hit the floor. In the ringing silence that followed, Smith pushed her father away, stepped back.

Then, belatedly, he bowed.

"The Donnell boy won," marveled one of the Comitatus men whom Arden didn't recognize. And another, "He *won?*"

Her father—her daddy—bowed back, both hands spread and empty. "Yes. Smith Donnell won."

"He did not!" That was Lowell, from beyond her father. "You threw the fight—didn't any of you see that? You let him win!"

"You can't know that, boy," warned Smith's father, bending to pick up the Civil War saber. "If Donaldson Leigh says he lost fair, he lost fair."

"But he didn't!" And then, as her own father turned to set his underling straight—

Too fast for Arden to react, Lowell surged at him.

Her father arched back in a sudden agony—and screamed.

Chapter 16

Even Smith didn't see it coming—and Smith had no illusions about Prescott Lowell's character.

Arden's father bellowed in pain and true surprise. Everyone pushed toward him. But Smith was closest.

He started forward even as Leigh's great, bearlike form collapsed to the marble floor, revealing Lowell behind him and the bloody, toothy knife in Lowell's red-stained hands. *He had to use both hands to pull it back out,* Smith thought numbly, automatically raising the Sword of Aeneas.

Lowell flipped the knife into his right hand, blade first, his gaze—and aim—seeking out Arden.

Smith ran him through with the Sword of Aeneas before he got any farther.

Antique as it was, the sword must have taken lives before, maybe in the hands of Hapsburgs, or Caesars or maybe even mythical Greek warriors. Smith hadn't. The reality of it shuddered through him. One minute, Lowell's eyes burned with the hatred of an egomaniac denied his illusion. The next, they had glazed over, and he was gone.

He slid heavily off Smith's flared blade as he dropped.

Smith would later figure that the shock made everything after that feel so...removed. Jeff screamed and threw himself onto Lowell's inert body, kicking and hitting, until Smith dragged him back. Arden fell to her knees beside her moaning father, snapped at Smith's dad to help turn him. Seeing the lake of blood forming beneath the big man's body, Jeff began to shudder in Smith's arms.

Arden pressed both hands over the spurting wound, poised and competent to the last.

And then Mitch and Val were there, appearing as if from nowhere, announcing that they'd called for an ambulance. Mitch stripped out of his latest guayabera, revealing a tank beneath, and gave the bunched material to Arden to help stop the blood.

"We've got it all on tape," he said softly to Smith after Jeff had deserted him to help his sister. "If you, you know... wondered. Lowell stabbed him before I could even drop the camera."

The words seemed far away. Even more surreal was Smith's father's command that everyone except him and the immediate family get the hell out of there and leave the matter to him.

"And how do you plan on explaining any of this to the cops?" demanded Val Diaz, not hiding her disgust at the afternoon's dealings.

"Let me handle the police," Will Donnell assured them. "The fewer witnesses they have to deal with, the more easily we can control this."

Heaven forbid word of this get out, right? Secrecy to the end.

Smith didn't bother hiding his scorn. "I don't need your protection."

His father glanced toward the broken Leigh family. "*They* do."

Still, Smith hesitated. It wasn't so much that he didn't trust his father with Arden anymore. One thing about Will Donnell—

he'd keep his promises, even to the extent of disowning his own son. The Comitatus belief in vows was part of what had caused all this. But Smith couldn't just *leave*.

"Arden…" he started.

But Arden herself disagreed, low-voiced, from her position over her dying father. "I thought you were trying to live off the grid," she spat.

Smith couldn't tell if it was an accusation or not. Now wasn't the time to care. He dropped onto one knee beside her, left the Sword of Aeneas forgotten on the floor—for her— and reached for the already bloody bandage of Mitch's shirt to help apply pressure. "I want to be here for you. Let me take over—"

"No!" Blood smeared the heart-shaped face she lifted to him. Her large eyes swam with tears. But her expression left no doubt. "Let me worry about Daddy without worrying about you, too, Smith. If the Comitatus owns the police…and nobody guaranteed your safety…just *get out of here!*"

He didn't want to leave her. God—anything else! But hadn't he just explained to her father that Arden was a free agent?

Arden spared him one last glare. "Take your damned sword and leave!"

"I'm…sorry." But Smith obediently curled his hand around his blade's grip, taking it up again, wiping Lowell's blood off on the leg of his jeans. He let Mitch and Val drag him back from the scene, holstering his revolver left-handed when Mitch gave it to him.

He felt himself die a little, inside, to leave the woman he loved all but weeping over the man who'd tried to betray her and then, ultimately, to save her. Because Leigh *had* thrown the fight. Smith knew that better than anyone.

He found he respected Leigh for the first time in years. For losing.

Losing for the right reason beat winning for the wrong one, every time.

Maybe that, thought Smith, was where the once heroic, once honorable Comitatus had gone wrong. They'd always won—until winning became everything. But nobody, nobody could count this as a win.

Leigh had grown unnaturally white as the blood beneath him pooled red.

Damned honor.

"Do you want to ride with your father?" the EMTs asked Arden as they wheeled her father's gurney toward the waiting ambulance.

Daddy's hand tightened on hers, his eyes unfocused over the oxygen mask. His blood smelled thick and wrong in the August heat.

Arden glanced at Jeff, where he stood lost at the edge of the drive. "No. I'll follow with my brother." No way would she leave Will Donnell to bring him—and she'd just sent away the only man she truly trusted. Maybe trusted. After having seen the extent of his secrets, and watched him skewer a man, she wasn't so sure.

Which hadn't meant she didn't want him out of there and safe.

Daddy's blue lips moved, blowing red bubbles in his attempt to speak.

Arden bent nearer.

"I'm sorry, bunny."

Was he? She wasn't sure it really mattered. Sorry or not, he'd threatened her life. Smith's life. And maybe worse, even if he'd never have gone through with any of that?

He'd risked turning Jeff into someone just like him.

In the end, the damage was done.

Arden pulled her bloody hand free of his and stepped back, letting Smith's father climb into the ambulance to accompany her father instead. Chin high against this next chapter in her surreal afternoon, she watched the ambulance head out, its lights and sirens warning all comers of its approach.

Only then, after the security gates closed behind it, did she open her arms to Jeff. He fell into her embrace, safe.

Mostly. She knew from her time with troubled teens what witnessing violence could do to a boy his age.

"I'm sorry," he whispered against her. "I should—should have told you."

"Told me what, Jeffie?"

"About the stupid society. About the knives. Some of the guys at camp—they weren't supposed to tell—it's all secret—but I was going to join as soon as I turned fifteen, so they figured it was okay. But it's not!"

Fifteen. She looked at him, so young and…unfinished. She tried to remember Smith at that age, but they'd avoided each other so adamantly back then. He'd been such a *boy,* wild and obnoxious and arrogant and…

Oh, mercy. Now that she was no longer a teenager herself, she recognized the behavior. Smith had nurtured a crush on her all along! But she'd only started to notice him that way after she'd bloomed into her own power, and after his own personality calmed down a little with adulthood.

The Comitatus gave me something to believe in, he'd said. *It gave me a direction. And your petty, power-hungry bullying took that away from me.*

But he'd lied. Yes, they'd apparently taken his money, his social standing. But he had rejected them first. *Smith* had sacrificed, when nobody else among her father's peers knew the meaning of the word. He'd been better than he'd thought, all along.

Any last resentment of him for having joined the Comitatus faded to nonexistence. She knew from Greta and Sibyl that the Comitatus was bigger than this small group, bigger than Texas, bigger than the country. She knew Smith remained exiled, hunted. But she did not, could not regret having spent last night with him, even if safety kept him away from now on.

"It will be okay, Jeff," she told her brother, kissing his black curls.

"No, it won't."

"Yes, it will, no matter what happens—because *you're* all right. You did the right thing. You protected me, despite that you could have sided with Daddy and the others. I'm so proud of you, for thinking for yourself. I'm so proud of you for being yourself, despite the consequences."

She could have been talking to someone else, too.

"I didn't fight him." Jeff's words came out muffled against her.

"There's more to life than fighting." She hoped. "Now— let's get cleaned up and go to the hospital."

Her brother drew away, scowled at her. "Why should we? I don't care what happens to him. Let him die."

Her heart threatened to break. Had the Comitatus and their violence already ruined him beyond saving? But no. He was just lashing out. Smith had survived the society for years, and he'd turned out all right.

Better than all right.

"You know why." She let her steady gaze challenge her brother's.

He ducked his head, kicked the ground. "Because it's the right thing to do?"

Arden hugged him again, holding back her tears. Ladies rarely cried in public. But maybe…

Maybe it *would* be all right, after all.

Smith had Mitch—and Val—drive him by their crappy hotel rooms first. He did what he could to finish cleaning Lowell's blood off the Sword of Aeneas en route. But now that the danger had passed, he had bigger concerns than this strange new bond between him and the weapon.

He wanted to clean up before he went by the hospital.

"—the movie wasn't just bootleg anime, but *bad* bootleg anime." Mitch was laughing as Smith came out of the moldy bathroom, wiped down and wearing a fresh shirt and jeans. "So every time the characters mentioned this legendary sword, the English subtitles called it a 'utensil.' The best I can guess is, the translators somehow went from sword to knife to utensil. 'Behold, the utensil of my father!' Isn't that a hoot?"

Val stared at him, not cracking a smile.

"I thought it was a hoot," insisted Mitch amiably.

Val moved her stare to Smith and deadpanned, "Nice place. Can we go now?"

Of course, it wasn't a nice place. Mitch had been right— it really did smell like feet. Smith picked up the oversized duffel bag he'd been using over the last year and shoved the plastic Ziploc with his toiletries into it. Then his dirty clothes, in a plastic grocery bag. Then he collected his clean clothes, and shoved them in, too.

"Uh-oh." Mitch stood, concern sobering his cheerful expression. "You're making time-to-leave-now motions. Val, why is he…? Never mind. Smith, why are you making time-to-leave-now motions?"

"Besides the obvious?" It wasn't like Smith had kept that much to carry, after losing his business, his condo, his cars.

Arden. He'd been right to break it off with her the moment he'd left the Comitatus. How could he stand losing her again now? Other than, you know, getting drunk, which was at best temporary.

Think about it later.

In went his laptop. In went the expandable folder with all his important papers—including, he knew, some well-worn pictures of a beautiful, green-eyed beauty queen with Irish-black hair and dimples.

"What makes now time to leave? We've got the proof we need to protect the comptroller. You won the duel. Arden, Jeff, even Greta should be okay, and Greta's place is now the ultimate base—no Comitatus allowed within five blocks."

Smith barked out a laugh. "Of course *you'd* think the Comitatus would keep their side of the bargain." Once the Stuarts learned of what had just happened, none of them would be safe.

"Why would Blondie here think that?" Val's sober gaze cut from Smith to Mitch and back.

Oops. *Because unlike the rest of us, Mitch is still close with his dad, who is of course Comitatus.* But Smith couldn't say any of that without breaking his stupid damned decade-old oath and outing his best friend. So he made do with a shrug, head duck and sulky, "*'Cause.*"

"Right," said Val. "So are we going to the hospital or not?"

Donaldson Leigh had been brought to Baylor Medical Center, one of the preeminent hospitals in the country. Smith knew that if he, or Mitch or Trace were hurt, they'd end up at Parkland, the county hospital. In only a year, he'd come to actively fear getting hurt especially because of the county hospitals, despite the earnest efforts of the underpaid workers who struggled against overwhelming obstacles to keep them open. Overcrowded and understaffed, the emergency waiting rooms would have teemed with every underinsured patient from the indigent to the struggling middle class.

More people than he could ever have imagined, before circumstances had forced him to join them.

Here at Baylor, though, the surgical waiting area offered wood-paneled walls, leather upholstered furniture, live plants and a flat-panel television. Arden and Jeff had the room almost exclusively to themselves.

"Tell her I'm here?" asked Smith, hesitating in the hallway outside. He'd had to come, but for all he knew, his presence would upset Arden and her brother more than ever.

"No," said Val, leaving him behind to go gather her friend into a supportive embrace. Smith envied that embrace. Like it mattered, who got to hold her when her father might be dying.

Smith stood in the half-open doorway. If he could be of any help at all, he had to be here for the woman he loved. But if he was going to hurt her—

Hurt her more, that is…

Maybe Val did whisper something to Arden. Or maybe Arden just sensed his presence. She looked up, met his concern with weary green eyes.

Eyes which hardened into emotionless poise.

She shook her head once, dismissing him—and turned back to her friend.

And…that was that. Smith backed away. Let the door swing closed. Bit back a soft curse and turned—

Nearly running into his father, who stood behind him, holding two foam cups of what smelled like coffee.

Will Donnell stared at Smith.

Smith stared at his dad—the man who'd gotten him into the Comitatus in the first place. The man who'd disowned him when he quit.

The man who very well might have helped Leigh sacrifice his own daughter, for mere rules or tradition.

He made a wide circle and headed for the elevators—but, to his surprise, his dad followed. "Smith!"

Smith slowed, turned. "What?"

"You don't want to know the prognosis?"

Smith shrugged. "None of my business. I stabbed the *other* guy, and I finished the job." Good. That sounded like he didn't even care, like the light going out in Lowell's eyes wouldn't haunt him.

To his surprise, his father shrugged back. "Lowell deserved killing."

"Tell that to his family."

"I plan to."

What—was that some kind of support? Smith snorted out a harsh laugh. "Like they'll listen to you."

"They'll have to." Will Donnell seemed to be searching his son for something, as if memorizing Smith's health, weight, mood. "Leigh's still in surgery, but the prognosis isn't good. His blood loss could leave him in a coma. I'm going to be sublord of the area Comitatus. Reporting directly to Stuart."

Ooh—to Stuart himself, huh? "Be sure to have a supersecret parade to celebrate."

"We'll honor the agreement on which you dueled," his father told him stiffly. "Arden and Jeff are free agents. The area for five blocks around Greta Kaiser's home will remain neutral ground, for as long as she lives. And we're dropping the campaign against Molly Johannes."

"Considering that we've got the entire afternoon's entertainment on tape, that's a smart move," agreed Smith.

His father blinked, startled at the threat—then shook his head, grinned. His grin slanted sideways a little, like Smith's. "You always were a troublemaker."

"That doesn't make me wrong about any of this," insisted Smith.

His father actually seemed to consider that. "Doesn't make you right, either. Not about the society, and not for Arden Leigh. I can hold up our end of the agreements you won, but that doesn't do anything for your safety, or your friends. Especially if you go public with any of this. I still can't acknowledge you. You're no good for her, now. You know that, don't you?"

Of course Smith knew it. He was no better for Arden than Aeneas had once proved to be for Dido, the heartbroken Phoenician queen of Carthage.

That didn't mean he had to like it.

"Tell Mom I said hi," he said—and left.

Just like Aeneas left.

Maybe that sword was meant for him, after all. But bonded or not, he didn't want it.

Greta didn't like this at all. "It's your sword now, Smith. You keep it."

"No." Smith had pushed the sword and its velvet bed away from him, across the coffee table. "I'm not Comitatus."

That again? "But you once were. You represent everything the Comitatus could be again. Perhaps *deserves* to be again."

"I'll keep it," offered Trace, lifting the sword and turning it in his hands. His presence in the parlor put their number at five. Boy-girl-boy-girl-boy. If Greta could still think of herself as a "girl."

"No," said Smith simply—this time to him. "*You* aren't Comitatus, either, remember?"

Trace made a rude, sulky noise.

"From what Mitch told us about the happenings at the Leigh estate, Smith, you and the sword have bonded," insisted Greta.

She couldn't see the annoyance in Smith's expression as he turned to face down his blond friend, but she could certainly hear it in his voice, despite the strain of a smile tightening his words. "I'm not sure I'd trust anything Mitch said about a supersecret society's supersecret meetings."

"I might have mentioned what could have happened at the hypothetical meeting of a hypothetical group called the Schmomitatus," admitted Mitch. And that was true. He'd delighted Greta and Sibyl, both, by skirting the edges of what could be confessed without breaking any assumed vows of secrecy.

Then Smith got back from the hospital and had to deal not just with Mitch and Trace, but with outsiders Greta and Sibyl crowded into the parlor as he tried to return her father's sword. Why couldn't he just accept it?

"First off," said Smith, as if reading her mind, "the sword belonged to your father. You've got to have some second or third cousins out there somewhere. A piece as important as that should follow some kind of bloodline."

Greta turned in the direction she'd noticed little Sibyl sitting. "Isn't that just like a man? As if bloodlines mattered."

Sibyl nodded.

"How'd this become anti-man?" demanded Smith, while Mitch asked, "Why wouldn't bloodlines matter? Trace, let me see that. It can't be that old."

Trace passed the sword over, and went back to the cookies Greta had set out.

"Men are significantly more likely to kill stepsons than birth sons." Sibyl, petting Dido as she talked, sounded as if she were reciting some kind of study or statistics. Maybe she was, at that. "Threatened by other men's seed."

"Hey!" protested Trace. "I'm trying to eat, here."

"Women are more likely to bond emotionally, even with foundlings," Sibyl continued. "Small children should be trained to approach females for assistance when lost, because of this. Perhaps the sword has been recast."

Smith sat forward, resting his elbows on his knees. "And that bloodline stuff's got to do with me taking the Sword of Aeneas how, exactly?"

"It's not as if Hephaestus gave it to his descendent, either," Greta reminded him gently—she liked to think this was exactly the same sword that had been forged millennia ago. Who knew what divine processes of metallurgy had been lost since then? "Or Achilles to his. If legend really does hold correctly."

"Yeah, well, maybe that's because they didn't have kids." Smith certainly had sounded downhearted since he'd gotten back from the hospital. "Aeneas may have been all about duty and heroism. But he sucked when it came to love. If the other two had much in common with him there…"

"No," noted Sibyl. "Both sired sons. Both had consorts. In the afterlife, Achilles married the daughter of King Agamemnon. Her father sacrificed her to the gods. Needed wind for the Greek armies to reach Troy. Achilles was pissed."

Ah—was that interest Greta noticed in Smith's more open posture? In the way his breathing changed?

Was *that* why he hadn't wanted the sword?

"And Hephaestus married Aphrodite, goddess of love. Pass a cookie?" asked Sibyl.

"Get your own damned cookie," said Trace.

Greta couldn't see whether Sibyl stuck her tongue out at the large man, but she clearly heard the raspberry Sibyl blew at him. And the one he blew back at her.

"Goddess of love, huh?" mused Smith. Surely he couldn't have missed the resemblance, after all those years. If ever Aphrodite had a surrogate on earth, it was Arden Leigh.

"Besides." Now Greta could deliver the coup de grâce. "You didn't ask three times."

"Okay, *what* is with the three-times business?"

"Legend holds," explained Greta, taking the sword from Mitch and holding it out to Smith, "that if something's truly worthwhile, it must be requested three times. Then it cannot be denied for any but the most dire of reasons."

"It's in all the fairy tales." Sibyl sighed as if disgusted with his ignorance, and stood. Dido stood quickly, as well, her chain collar rattling with the movement. "I have to go now. Thank you for the food and shelter and…all."

"Wait," protested Trace, straightening on the love seat. *"What?"*

Even Mitch asked, "Where are you going?"

The young woman made a motion Greta interpreted as a shrug, bent to kiss Dido on the head one more time—and walked out, simple as that.

"Is it just my imagination?" asked Mitch. "Or is that girl—"

"Weird," agreed Smith.

"Unique," suggested Greta.

Trace shrugged. "Short."

"Okay." Mitch helped himself to a cookie. "As long as it's not just me."

To Greta's relief, Smith took the Sword of Aeneas from her hands and turned it, slowly. Eventually he stood, swished it through the air and nodded.

"Okay. As long as you asked nicely. Three times."

Greta beamed, delighted with how this last stage of her life was turning out.

Every leader needed a special sword.

At first, Arden told herself that her other responsibilities kept her away from Smith. She spent more time at the hospital than home those first few days until her father's vital signs stabilized. His vital signs, but not consciousness. The doctors doubted he would ever emerge from his coma.

Then she had to deal with the family attorneys, making arrangements for her father's long-term care, for Jeff's future, for the help's continued employment. She didn't miss the irony that her father hadn't gotten around to changing his power of attorney after he'd turned on her. Better for Jeff that way, though. Only once he was old enough, and ready, would she hand everything over to him.

Then of course came the social calls—not making them, but receiving them. Flowers and teacups and air kisses and coffee cakes. When one couldn't do anything else, one brought food and sympathy. Arden understood that.

But almost a week after her father's "accident," as the public version of the story somehow labeled it, Arden closed the door behind her latest clutch of visitors, leaned back against it and gave up. No more. Just…no more.

Jeff was at a friend's house. Visiting hours at the hospital were over. Thank-you cards could wait.

She had to find out whether Smith had left. Of course, part of her hoped he had. She'd told him to, hadn't she? Killing a Comitatus member couldn't have done anything to improve his safety, and clearly, many of the people in her own social circle were Comitatus. And yet...

Sugar. Selfish or not, she could barely breathe at the thought that he was gone. A year ago, she would have loved the image of *her* sending *him* away, to get back for the way he'd dumped her.

But either one of those scenarios still ended with them apart.

She didn't dare telephone him—what if her phone was bugged, and the Comitatus somehow traced him through her? She didn't know where he'd been staying all this time.

But Greta might. And the Comitatus already knew about Greta.

Arden drove to Greta's house.

Her heart cramped to see the fire damage to Greta's tree, visible even in the shadows of twilight, and the smoke stains on her house—how could she have been so self-involved as to forget what Smith had said about a fire? But it beat faster when she recognized Mitch's primer-gray car in the driveway.

It beat even faster when the front door opened, letting out the sound of Dido's barking—and one Smith Donnell, whole and healthy and *there*.

Still there.

Even better, he opened his arms for her. She ran to his embrace—and everything was right again.

At least, momentarily right.

But so much was involved now, besides them. She forced herself to look up, when all she wanted was to stay in his arms forever. "Are we safe out here? Is there anyone with Comitatus connections around? Other than you, I mean."

Smith neither confirmed nor denied—but he didn't have to. She'd seen him fight a duel for her. She'd heard him bargain for her life as no outsider could have done. She knew.

"We're fine," he assured her—and she trusted his word and his abilities wholly, knew it must be true. "For now. I heard about your father, Ard. I'm sorry. Is there any…?"

It sounded too much like the sympathy visits she'd been fielding all week. "Not really, no. Thank you for…for asking…."

Which is when her mask crumbled. She fell into him in sudden, uncontrolled desperation. Again he enfolded her in his strong arms, drew her tight against him as she broke down in sobs. Her father had betrayed her and now lay in a terrible limbo, neither alive nor dead. His estate lay in her hands, and she had no idea if she could handle it. She'd been beaten, lied to, imprisoned. She'd seen her lover kill someone, though that someone had deserved it. Her whole world felt like a lie.

All of it, that is, except for Smith.

He smelled of salt, fresh lumber, dust—and *him*. He felt…

He felt like everything good in the world. Like security and safety. Like home. How could she bear it, when she knew he might never be safe with her, when she knew…

"Shh." He kissed her hair, her cheeks, her eyes, not seeming to care how terrible she must look. "Arden, darling. I know, sweetness. I know. Let it out."

And she did, her usual composure dissolving into nothing but despair and tears and confusion. Finally she could cry no more. She realized, more slowly than she should, that she was sitting on his lap. He'd settled onto the front porch, under the half-charred oak tree. In sight of the whole neighborhood. And it didn't matter.

Only then did she recognize what he kept saying, over and over again. "I'm sorry, darling. I'm sorry. I'm—"

Her laugh came out unfortunately wet. "Whatever have *you* got to be sorry about?"

"I brought this crap down on you. I—"

But she pressed a hand to his mouth, unable to bear the shame that shadowed his handsome face. "No. I'd started looking into the Comitatus for Greta before you ever came back. This isn't your fault—mostly it's Prescott Lowell's. A lot of it's Daddy's, and the rest of the Comitatus. *Not you.*"

He simply gazed at her, so close, so…there. She watched him in the yellow of the porch light, admiring his jaw, his cheekbones, his now-solemn brown eyes. Only when she realized that he was watching her in the same way did she consider how terrible she must look after her crying jag.

Quickly she turned away from him, covered her face with her hands, tried to wipe away any possible smears of mascara—or anything else. "I must look a mess! My makeup, and my hair, and…"

To her surprise, he drew her face back to him and kissed her. Deeply. She fell into it, into him, lips to lips, soul to soul. Yes…

Only when they stopped, just to catch their breath, did she blink at him in sleepy surprise.

"I love you messy," he explained, punctuating his words by kissing up her jaw. "I love it when you let down your prize-winning comportment and I get to see the real you."

"The comportment is the real me." But she couldn't make a terribly convincing argument, lifting her chin to grant him delicious access to her neck—and sniffing back more tears.

"I love her, too. But the messy Arden is the you under even that. The one not everyone gets to see."

She arched into his lovemaking, which reminded her of other things only he got to see. And how much she'd loved having him back in her life.

And how much it would hurt to lose him again. But she had to.

It was the one thing she had to do for him. The one sacrifice that was truly hers to make.

If she let this—oh, yes, especially that bit with his tongue—go on much longer, she would lose her nerve. So she wove her fingers into his hair and somehow, instead of drawing him to her, managed to push him away. "You need to go."

He blinked sleepily at her. "What?"

"Please."

"For how long?"

She'd expected him to behave like a gentleman and simply accept her decision…but this was Smith. "Long enough. I don't know. Forever, if that's what it takes to keep you out of the way of the Comitatus."

Slowly, Smith's agonized expression relaxed. He seemed to sag in relief—relief!—until his drooping head came to rest on her shoulder.

"Please, Smith. If we wait much longer, I won't be able to say goodbye."

"Darn," he said, and kissed her cheek.

Arden felt herself stiffen. Darn? Here she was, trying to do the honorable thing, and he said *darn?*

She tried to push him back from her, palms on his hard shoulders. "I asked you to leave, Mr. Donnell." But she couldn't manage quite the arch tone she normally did. Maybe because of the congestion.

"Now it's Mr. Donnell?" He was laughing at her! Well, his eyes were laughing. His mouth seemed to fight a losing battle against a grin. "No."

"No?"

"I'm not leaving you." Apparently he did a mental double check at that, because he quickly added, "Not unless you've got a much better reason than protecting me."

"Excuse me?"

"You're excu— Oof!" Arden herself wasn't sure if she'd

hit him on purpose or by accident as she stood from his lap. Well, he'd said he liked seeing her without her social niceties.

So she said, "If I remember correctly, you left *me* for *my* protection, you ass!" This time, she managed exactly the right note of disdain.

"Well, I was wrong."

She stared at him. "Say that again."

He tipped his head back, his brown eyes more honest than she'd ever seen—except maybe when they'd shared a bed. "I was wrong, Arden. I was stupid, and proud and chauvinistic. I shouldn't have been such a coward as to break up with you over the phone."

She swallowed, hard. "Drunk," she reminded him. But the outrage was gone, leaving only worry. Only…hope.

"Drunk. No matter what I maybe couldn't tell you, I should have tried harder to tell you *something*." Now he stood, and stepped close, almost against her. Brave man. Her foolishly brave Smith. "I should have told you how incredible you are. I should have told you that any man would be downright blessed to have you. I should have told you that I would be miserable every damned day without you."

She would be miserable every day without him, too. "Well…then I would have wanted to know why you were leaving me, if I were so special."

"And I would've said, 'Just one of those things.'"

She rolled her eyes, ladylike or not. "And I would probably have hit you."

"And I would have enjoyed it, because I love it when you're not being a lady." He put a hand on each of her shoulders, held her safe. "Dad gave Greta's house safe status, Ard. Mitch and I are going to stay here, make Dallas a kind of base, see if we convince more secret-society members to see the error of their ways. Maybe we can help turn them honorable again. Now, if you honestly don't want to be with me, I'll understand. I might whine and complain and stalk you a little, maybe, but I'll understand. We'll all be taking some risk, standing up to the society elders. You've already got one loved one in the hospital, so if you just can't take on the stress of worrying about me…that's your call. But if you want to do the best thing for me? *Don't leave me.* Don't make me leave you."

"I…don't want you to get hurt because of me."

"Yeah, and I don't want you or Jeff hurt because I'm not there to help. But we all get to decide what to risk our lives on, right? A certain secret society—let's call it the Schmomitatus—once gave me something to believe in." He studied her, up and down, and finally she didn't worry about what she looked like. She had the feeling he was seeing past that, anyway. He was seeing her.

He found her beautiful for more than her appearance.

"Now *you* give me that," he said simply. And her heart cracked—not with misery, but joy. She felt too much joy to hold it all in. "Look, Ard. It's not like I have much to offer. Not even complete safety—"

"Shut up." And she kissed him.

"Yes, ma'am," he murmured, sexily, against her lips. Then he scooped her into his arms. She squealed, then clutched around his neck and held on for dear life. She had a feeling she'd be doing that—really and metaphorically—quite a bit around Smith and his secret-society exiles.

But it was, she consoled herself, most *definitely* the right thing to do.

* * * * *

Don't miss the next Blade Keepers romance,
Sibyl and Trace's story,
UNDERGROUND WARRIOR,
coming soon.
Only from Evelyn Vaughn
and Silhouette Romantic Suspense!

*Celebrate 60 years of pure reading pleasure
with Harlequin®!*

*Harlequin Presents® is proud to introduce
its gripping new miniseries,*
THE ROYAL HOUSE OF KAREDES.
*An exquisite coronation diamond, split as a symbol of a
warring royal family's feud, is missing! But whoever
reunites the diamond halves will rule all....*

*Welcome to eight brand-new titles that unfold to reveal the
stories of kings and queens, princes and princesses torn
apart by pride and power, but finally reunited by love.*

*Step into the world of Karedes with
BILLIONAIRE PRINCE, PREGNANT MISTRESS.
Available July 2009
from Harlequin Presents®.*

ALEXANDROS KAREDES, SNOW DUSTING the shoulders of his leather jacket and glittering like jewels in his dark hair, stood at the door. Maria felt the blood drain from her head.

"Good evening, Ms. Santos."

His voice was as she remembered it. Deep. Husky. Perfect English, but with the faintest hint of a Greek accent. And cold, as cold as it had been that awful morning she would never forget, when he'd accused her of horrible things, called her terrible names....

"Aren't you going to ask me in?"

She fought for composure. Last time they'd faced each other, they'd been on his turf. Now they were on hers. She was in command here, and that meant everything.

"There's a sign on the door downstairs," she said, her tone every bit as frigid as his. "It says, 'No soliciting or vagrants.'"

His lips drew back in a wolfish grin. "Very amusing."

"What do you want, Prince Alexandros?"

A tight smile eased across his mouth and it killed her that even now, knowing he was a vicious, arrogant man, she couldn't help but notice what a handsome mouth it was. Chiseled. Generous. Beautiful, like the rest of him, which made him living proof that beauty could, indeed, be only skin deep.

"Such formality, Maria. You were hardly so proper the last time we were together."

She knew his choice of words was deliberate. She felt her face heat; she couldn't help that but she damned well didn't have to let him lure her into a verbal sparring match.

"I'll ask you once more, your highness. What do you want?"

"Ask me in and I'll tell you."

"I have no intention of asking you in. Tell me why you're here or don't. It's your choice, just as it will be my choice to shut the door in your face."

He laughed. It infuriated her but she could hardly blame him. He was tall—six two, six three—and though he stood with one shoulder leaning against the door frame, hands tucked casually into the pockets of the jacket, his pose was deceptive. He was strong, with the leanly muscled body of a well-trained athlete.

She remembered his body with painful clarity. The feel of him under her hands. The power of him moving over her. The taste of him on her tongue.

Suddenly, he straightened, his laughter gone. "I have not come this distance to stand in your doorway," he said coldly, "and I am not going to leave until I am ready to do so. I suggest you stand aside and stop behaving like a petulant child."

A petulant child? Was that what he thought? This man who had spent hours making love to her and had then accused her of—of trading her body for profit?

Except it had not been love, it had been sex. And the sooner she got rid of him, the better.

She let go of the doorknob and stepped aside. "You have five minutes."

He strolled past her, bringing cold air and the scent of the night with him. She swung toward him, arms folded. He reached past her, pushed the door closed, then folded his arms, too. She wanted to open the door again but she'd be damned if she was going to get into a who's-in-charge-here argument with him. She was in charge, and he would surely see a tussle over the ground rules as a sign of weakness.

Instead, she looked past him at the big clock above her worktable.

"Ten seconds gone," she said briskly. "You're wasting time, your highness."

"What I have to say will take longer than five minutes."

"Then you'll just have to learn to economize. More than five minutes, I'll call the police."

Instantly, his hand was wrapped around her wrist. He tugged her toward him, his dark-chocolate eyes almost black with anger.

"You do that and I'll tell every tabloid shark I can contact about how Maria Santos tried to buy a five-hundred-thousand-dollar commission by seducing a prince." He smiled thinly. "They'll lap it up."

* * * * *

What will it take for this billionaire prince to realize
he's falling in love with his mistress…?
Look for
BILLIONAIRE PRINCE, PREGNANT MISTRESS
by Sandra Marton.
Available July 2009
from Harlequin Presents®.

We'll be spotlighting a different series every month
throughout 2009 to celebrate our 60th anniversary.

Look for Harlequin® Presents in July!

TWO CROWNS, TWO ISLANDS, ONE LEGACY

A royal family, torn apart by pride and its lust for
power, reunited by purity and passion

Step into the world of Karedes
beginning this July with

BILLIONAIRE PRINCE,
PREGNANT MISTRESS
by

Sandra Marton

Eight volumes to collect and treasure!

REQUEST YOUR FREE BOOKS!

2 FREE NOVELS PLUS 2 FREE GIFTS!

Silhouette® Romantic

SUSPENSE

Sparked by Danger, Fueled by Passion!

YES! Please send me 2 FREE Silhouette® Romantic Suspense novels and my 2 FREE gifts (gifts are worth about $10). After receiving them, if I don't wish to receive any more books, I can return the shipping statement marked "cancel." If I don't cancel, I will receive 4 brand-new novels every month and be billed just $4.24 per book in the U.S. or $4.99 per book in Canada. That's a savings of at least 15% off the cover price! It's quite a bargain! Shipping and handling is just 50¢ per book*. I understand that accepting the 2 free books and gifts places me under no obligation to buy anything. I can always return a shipment and cancel at any time. Even if I never buy another book from Silhouette, the two free books and gifts are mine to keep forever.

240 SDN EYL4 340 SDN EYMG

Name _____ (PLEASE PRINT) _____

Address _____ Apt. # _____

City _____ State/Prov. _____ Zip/Postal Code _____

Signature (if under 18, a parent or guardian must sign) _____

Mail to the **Silhouette Reader Service:**
IN U.S.A.: P.O. Box 1867, Buffalo, NY 14240-1867
IN CANADA: P.O. Box 609, Fort Erie, Ontario L2A 5X3

Not valid to current subscribers of Silhouette Romantic Suspense books.

Want to try two free books from another line?
Call 1-800-873-8635 or visit www.morefreebooks.com.

* Terms and prices subject to change without notice. Prices do not include applicable taxes. Sales tax applicable in N.Y. Canadian residents will be charged applicable provincial taxes and GST. Offer not valid in Quebec. This offer is limited to one order per household. All orders subject to approval. Credit or debit balances in a customer's account(s) may be offset by any other outstanding balance owed by or to the customer. Please allow 4 to 6 weeks for delivery. Offer available while quantities last.

Your Privacy: Silhouette is committed to protecting your privacy. Our Privacy Policy is available online at www.eHarlequin.com or upon request from the Reader Service. From time to time we make our lists of customers available to reputable third parties who may have a product or service of interest to you. If you would prefer we not share your name and address, please check here. ☐

SRS09R

Do you crave dark and sensual paranormal tales?

Get your fix with Silhouette Nocturne!

In print:
Two new titles available every month wherever books are sold.

Online:
Nocturne eBooks available monthly from **www.silhouettenocturne.com**.

Nocturne Bites:
Short sensual paranormal stories available monthly online from **www.nocturnebites.com** and in print with the Nocturne Bites collections available April 2009 and October 2009 wherever books are sold.

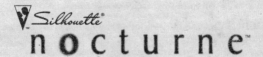

www.silhouettenocturne.com
www.paranormalromanceblog.com

SNBITESRG

Romantic
SUSPENSE

COMING NEXT MONTH

Available June 30, 2009

#1567 THE UNEXPECTED HERO—Rachel Lee
Conard County: The Next Generation
Newly returned from nursing in V.A. hospitals, Kristin Tate clashes
with Dr. David Marcus on her first shift at Community Hospital. Yet
clearly there's an attraction beneath the surface. And when two patients
mysteriously die on her shift, rag dolls left as a killer's signature, David is
determined to prove Kristin's innocence…or die trying.

#1568 PRINCE CHARMING FOR 1 NIGHT—Nina Bruhns
Love in 60 Seconds
To secure the return of his family's recently stolen diamond ring,
Conner Rothchild must use exotic dancer Vera Mancuso as bait for the real
thief—and not let her out of his sight. During their crash course on social
graces, he finds himself wanting her, and the feeling is mutual. But when a
cold-blooded killer kidnaps Vera, can Conner save her?

#1569 TERMS OF ATTRACTION—Kylie Brant
Alpha Squad
Blackmailed into joining a foreign president's security detail, Ava Carter
finds herself at odds with protection specialist Cael McCabe. Quickly onto
her duplicity, Cael still can't resist the heat that sizzles between them as
they track down a kidnapper deep in the South American jungles. But the
biggest risk of all will be trusting each other with their hearts.

#1570 MEDUSA'S MASTER—Cindy Dees
H.O.T. Watch
Someone is stealing priceless art from Caribbean mansions, and Special
Forces soldiers Katrina Kim and Jeff Steiger must find out who it is.
Sparks fly immediately, but as Kat comes face-to-face with the thief, they
discover an even bigger threat. With Kat now in the line of fire, can Jeff
live with the risks she takes in her work and find a way to love all of her?

SRSCNMBPA0609